make
believe
love

make believe love

a novel by Lee Gowan

ALFRED A. KNOPF CANADA

PUBLISHED BY ALFRED A. KNOPF CANADA

Copyright © 2001 by Lee Gowan

All rights reserved under International and Pan-American Copyright
Conventions. Published in 2001 by Alfred A. Knopf Canada, a division
of Random House of Canada Limited, Toronto. Distributed by
Random House of Canada Limited, Toronto.

Knopf Canada and colophon are trademarks.

~

Canadian Cataloguing in Publication Data

Gowan, Lee, 1961-
Make believe love

ISBN 0-676-97286-1

I. Title.

PS8563.O882M34 2001   C813'.54   C00-932419-4
PR9199.3.G68M34 2001

~

FIRST EDITION

Visit Random House of Canada Limited's Web site: www.randomhouse.ca

Printed and bound in the United States of America

10 9 8 7 6 5 4 3 2 1

For Alison, Adam, and Riley
And in Memory of Jerry and Fahey

When you are old and grey and full of sleep,
And nodding by the fire, take down this book,
And slowly read, and dream of the soft look
Your eyes had once, and of their shadows deep.

W.B. YEATS

The crowd which the seeker after fame envisages
consists of shadows; that is, of creatures who
do not even have to be alive so long as they are
capable of one thing, which is to repeat his name.

ELIAS CANETTI
Crowds and Power

make
believe
love

I f you drive west on the Trans-Canada Highway, through a million miles of Precambrian Shield, the great red rocks clawing straight through the earth to confront you with the fact you've already crossed beyond the beginnings of your kind and into the lush and smoky world before history; and yet you keep driving, winding your way west to where the land flattens and trees begin losing ground to clearings where farms and tractors hold what can only be temporary dominion over the great forest; and still you drive, until you find yourself passing through the most relentless landscape on the face of the planet, burnt grass and stubble and assorted shades of brown stretching away on either side of a highway that runs straight into the sky, the blinking yellow centre line threatening to murder you by hypnotizing you into a messy sleep; and yet you persist in your going, perhaps deluded into believing you have reached the unfinished edge of the world and are about to make a significant discovery by dropping into the abyss that Columbus's crew so *greatly feared—if you drive west on the Trans-Canada Highway, eventually you'll come to a spot on the map called Broken Head, Saskatchewan, just another Prairie town dying from complete lack of culture and too much interbreeding, a place with absolutely no significance beyond the fact that Darwin Andrew Goodwin once picked up his mail at the post office on Main Street.*

And if—perhaps after a lunch of deep-fried breaded meat and lumpy gravy and powdered mashed potatoes slopped onto a cold plate and shared with a waitress who insists on telling you all about her children's latest diseases or the plot of her favourite soap opera—if you then head south on a secondary highway, away from the last vestiges of what some might laughably refer to as civilization, and you turn west again on the Hochfeld Grid, named for a disappeared community of Mennonite settlers who, a century ago, were conned by the Canadian government into coming to this godforsaken place, you will be following the same route that RCMP Detectives Brock and Frazier took on the morning of May 12th, 199–, when they arrived with a search warrant at the Goodwin farm to seek out documentary evidence that would prove Darwin Andrew Goodwin had murdered Stephanie Rush.

What they found was the Goodwin forest: acres and acres of Scotch pines planted in a grid of squares measuring exactly a hundred yards on each side. (Goodwin was never an advocate of the metric system.) A driveway bisecting the rigidly ordered

*woods led the two officers into a kind of courtyard in the cen-
tre, where a few corrugated steel sheds were surrounded by rows
of antiquated machinery, the parts supply for the ancient com-
bine harvester and swather and tractors that Goodwin still used
to farm the land he hadn't already turned over to the trees.
When the detectives walked through one of these coniferous
walls they found a hundred square yards of open clearing, overgrown with dead grass and weeds. They stood for a moment,
looking around. The space the trees created gave them an eerie
feeling of being audience to nothing in an empty and unused
arena.*

*They did not realize they were witnessing evidence of
Goodwin's great love for Stephanie Rush—Hollywood sex sym-
bol, tabloid icon of the seventies, the Province of Alberta's most
celebrated daughter—who had so recently and cruelly passed
from this vale of tears. Goodwin planted the trees for her: as
spokeswoman for the Sierra Club, Stephanie Rush had urged
him, in countless thirty-second spots, to do his part to help save
the rain forest.*

*Investigating further, they found another square of pines
occupied by a decaying farmhouse. As they climbed the front
steps Detective Brock's foot broke through the top plate, and
Detective Frazier remembers him limping slightly for the rest of
the day. Their knock brought no response, but upon entering
they were attacked by an elderly woman their report describes
as "armed with a television antenna of the rabbit ears variety."*

The woman, Goodwin's mother, was raving about aliens from other planets preparing to take over the world.

Again the detectives missed the clue. Stephanie Rush was originally from Venus, a village in Alberta.

Having concluded that questioning Mrs. Goodwin would be fruitless, the detectives made a tactical retreat. They stood in the yard, surveyed the situation, and noticed a telephone line running from the southwesterly corner of the house off into the woods; not toward the road, as you would expect, but in the opposite direction. A single wire was strung on either side of each pole, the lines attached to each cross arm at a green glass insulator. These rows of crucifixes once filed in procession along seemingly every Prairie road, but they had completely disappeared when all the phone lines were buried by SaskTel over a decade before.

Following the line a quarter of a mile through four or five squares of pines—some of them completely empty, some storing scrap metal or more rusting machinery or piles of weathered lumber—the detectives discovered the end of the line at a prefab bungalow that would not have looked out of place in any suburb in Middle America. What made it look out of place in that particular clearing—what might have made it remind them of the cottage that Hansel and Gretel stumbled across, though it was not made of gingerbread—was that it was so well tended: recently painted, and the flowerbeds all weeded and groomed. A white picket fence marked the boundaries of a perfect green lawn.

On this occasion Detectives Brock and Frazier did not over-look the evidentiary significance of their find: they realized at once that this was the legendary house Goodwin had built for Stephanie Rush; as such, it could well prove important to their mission of gathering documentation, circumstantial or otherwise, that would link Mr. Goodwin to Ms. Rush's untimely passing.

What the good detectives had certainly not expected to find—what indeed seemed to be a substantial impediment to their mission—was that the woman's face they spotted in the green-shuttered window, peering out at them as she washed the lunch dishes, was instantly recognizable from a trillion photos as the face of Stephanie Rush.

An excerpt from
Make Believe Love
by Jason Warwick

[Saturday, June 10th]

It's true that the place I come from isn't
fashionable or pretty, but Jason Warwick
has no right to insult it. He's never actually seen the Prairie.
Yes, he lived here for a little while, but he can't see anything that hasn't been packaged and labelled, and the place
I come from doesn't fit inside a frame.

   On my parents' wedding day, for instance, you'll notice
the bridal party clustered in the bottom of the photo, their
peach dresses cut off by the white Kodak border at their
knees, so that you can't help searching for what exactly it is
you're supposed to be focusing on up over their plastic sun
hats in the huge expanse of cloudless blue sky. If she were
not there, grinning painfully in her white gown in the centre of that party, I would suspect that my mother had taken
the photo herself. Come to think of it, though, her spe-
cialty was cutting off my *head*, leaving my frilly pink torso,
white stockings, and buckled shiny black shoes floating
above a brown lawn or a dusty stretch of earth. Sometimes,

in the best ones, you can pick out the shapes of pebbles that have long ago been lost underground.

My father is missing from all of their wedding photos. A few snaps exist of him and Mom brushing confetti from their shoulders on the front steps of the church, immediately following the ceremony, but you won't find him in any of the posed efforts taken in Memorial Park, the cenotaph to the war dead looming behind my mother's cousin Ernie, the inept photographer, as he manipulated the shutter. Dad was supposed to be there, but after the vows the best man spirited him away for a quick drink, and by the time he reappeared he was so wasted my mother wouldn't allow him to ruin his own reception. Dad insists he really wasn't very drunk—that Mom only wanted to create a scandal as revenge for his being late for the photo session, which is entirely possible, knowing my mother. At any rate, they argued for a while, but there was only one possible outcome to my parents' arguments, and in the end he slouched off to wait for her in their motel room on the service road, while she went and offered their guests his regrets, explaining he'd suddenly been taken ill.

You won't see me in the photograph, either, but I am there, the prime force behind the momentous occasion, and I can remember it all perfectly: my mother grimly insisting that they couldn't wait for my father any longer, as her bridesmaids and Uncle Ernie and her parents all desperately tried to calm her and convince her that there was no need to hurry, he'd probably be along any minute now. Mom would have none of it, demanding to be taken home to rest before the reception, and then squashing any possible resistance by seating herself on the steps of the cenotaph and declaring, "I feel as though I'm about to have the baby right here."

Her parents rushed her off to her own bedroom, where Dad caught up to her a half hour later, but was only admitted after an hour of negotiations through the locked door.

I wasn't born for another six months.

I have too many of these phantom, impossible memories, and I hold the camera lens responsible. My mother was constantly looking for some way to express herself, and photography was an easy way to pretend she was doing so. She was an only child, and her parents praised anything she did so far beyond its merits that she soon lost all capacity for embarrassment. Our living-room walls were covered with flat two-dimensional landscapes she'd painted when she was a teenager: canvases that I imagine must roughly depict the prairie as Jason Warwick sees it. After I was born she gave up painting for photography, snapping photos of me in gaudy frilly dresses she'd designed and sewn herself. I'd pose and she'd scold me with "Act like a lady." Whatever that was. I soon discovered she was after mincing, not vamping. She'd enter these images—the better ones, containing a head and most of my other body parts—in any photography contest that had the misfortune of coming to her attention. The fact that she never won a prize only made her bitterly suspicious of an elaborate elitist conspiracy to overlook her talents.

To make matters worse, someone gave my parents a Super 8 camera for a wedding present. Consequently, I remember all of the vital events of my first three years happening in full-colour silence: there I am, naked, looking for all the world like an alien or a live roast as my father lowers me into the kitchen sink for my first bath, and there I am drooling on my first birthday cake, and there's the moment I took my first step, pushing away the chair I'd been using for a walker and watching it clatter to the floor without a sound. I applaud ecstatically until I lose my balance and land plop on my bum. I've seen it so many times I swear I can actually remember the humiliation I project into those terrible tears.

Things changed shortly after I turned three. My mother bought herself a portable video camera—they were just becoming affordable at the time—and suddenly my memories have sound: my fourth birthday, my fifth Christmas, my fifth Valentine's day, my fifth Easter Sunday, my brother's third birthday, my first swimming lesson, my first day of kindergarten, my fifth birthday, my sixth Christmas....

There is a full sixty-minute tape of my first dance lesson and I have watched every moment: every grimace, every self-conscious flick of my hair, every shy peek at the other girls to see how they bounce when the teacher says to push right down through the floor. It was also my last dance lesson. I felt so clumsy and stupid I refused to go again.

All of this may seem trivial to you, but a serious violation took place in those miles and miles of footage. For one thing, it's very difficult for me to identify actual memories of my childhood. Most of my authentic experiences have been recorded over by those videotapes. Worse still, even now, as I sit at this desk writing these words, I can't help watching myself seated here—can't help pulling myself up a little straighter, then purposely slouching, then hiding my face in my hands. And it's always been this way. I've experienced too much of life with the feeling that the world I walk through is simply a quaint representation of what the world must really be like. No matter what I do, I can't seem to escape the frame my mother composed so sloppily around me.

Which is why I've decided to write this to you, despite the fact that I really don't have the time. One week. That's all I can spare. The earth won't wait any longer than a week, so I've got to get this down fast and be done with it. But let me make one thing perfectly clear: these words are much more than a response to Jason Warwick's ridiculous book. I am telling my story in hopes of freeing Goodwin, but also to free myself. Somewhere beyond the Joan Swift created by my mother's challenged lenses and Jason Warwick's pitiful brain, there must be a real live human being.

And I have a whole week to discover her.

My first actual un-document-inspired memory came in a fever brought on by an abscessed tooth. I recall it as a summer night, one of those stiflingly heavy nights that follow days when the wind has blown since sunrise, as though God were using His or Her or Its electric hairdryer to atomize the last stubborn droplet of moisture from the cracked and doomed earth. To be honest, I'm not really sure it was summer at all: my own overheated, dehydrated state may have made me imagine it that way. By the time my mother flicked on my bedroom light to see what I was moaning about, my temperature was nearly 105 and my sheets were so soggy she claimed she could have wrung enough salt water from them to start a new ocean—an inland sea, the Joanatic Ocean—right there, in the middle of the prairie.

She peeled off my pink cotton nightie, dunked me in a cool bath, and while I screamed bloody murder, she knelt beside me on the floor, murmuring that she'd warned me, hadn't she, what would happen if I didn't brush my teeth before bed. "I told you, didn't I, Joan? You keep up this way and you'll end up like one of those toothless old maids in the city, begging for coins by the bus stop."

In all probability, these words were not so much meant for me as for my father, standing silently in the doorway, waiting for the order to rush me off to the hospital. A moment later my mother turned to him and said, "I hope that car's working when we need it for once, because if it's not, then I hate to consider the consequences."

The family car was a sporty model left over from my father's single days. A Plymouth Roadrunner. Its absurdly long hood hid an engine that might have been big enough to make our tractor redundant. My brother and I loved it for its horn, which beeped like its cartoon namesake, but my mother hated every metal inch of it as though it were one of Dad's former girlfriends, and she used any tiny malfunction as an excuse to lobby for a new car more appropriate to the needs of a growing family.

Dad offered to carry me, but Mom would have none of that. She pulled a clean nightie over my head, and cradling me in her arms, struggled down the stairs and out the door and across the yard to where her mechanical nemesis waited under the fingernail moon. The crickets sang the same old song they always sing.

"You know why this happened, don't you?" Mom asked.

"She never brushed her teeth?" Dad responded as he attempted to balance Brian—who hadn't even woken when he was scooped from his bed—in the crook of his arm at the same time as he pulled open the passenger door and propped the seat forward to let Mom and me in.

"Fluoride. Your stupid well has no fluoride in it. We might as well be living in darkest Africa." With that, she slid in the back and waited for him to slam the door behind her.

The engine caught immediately. Dad patted the dashboard and murmured, "Good girl." Mom was silent for a few miles.

I remember lying there, resting my head on my mother's lap, staring at what I could see of the dashboard between the bucket seats, listening to Brian's stuffed nose whistle as he snored and the gravel popping against the bottom of the car.

"She's burning up," my mother whimpered as we turned north, toward Broken Head, at Goodwin's forest, "and here we are in the middle of nowhere. She'll likely be dead by the time we get to town."

This time Dad did not respond.

I still have that molar, its roots craggy and twisted as an old oak's, the crown blasted the colour of charcoal, as if a firestorm had passed through my mouth.

For Mom, my blackened enamel and inflamed gums were another sign of a world gone rotten, and there weren't many of the world's problems that couldn't be traced back to the four square miles of rolling creek valley and sandy soil my father inherited when his father dropped dead of a heart attack at forty-eight, a self-made man with clogged arteries.

How do I describe the farm to you without imagining Jason rolling his eyes up in his bored, oh, so cosmopolitan way?

Our farm was an accumulation of many farms: there was the Vaughn place, the Anderson place, the Davies place, the Thomas place, and if you walked any of these quarter sections and you knew where to look among the rosebushes and the wolf willow, you would find a depression in the ground and maybe a bit of the stone foundation that marked where the Vaughns or the Davieses or the Thomases had tried to invent themselves, before the Dust Bowl finally choked them out. If you dug around, you might discover shards of pottery, or blackened tin cans. My father had found some scattered silverware on the Davies homestead and wondered how they could possibly have forgotten what must have been among their most valuable possessions, but I liked to imagine Mrs. Davies tossing the silver over her shoulder as she walked away forever from the shack she'd called home.

My father also found arrowheads and stone awls and scrapers in our fields or lying in the middle of trails where our wheels had worn away the prairie wool. And at the edge of the Anderson place, on a ridge above where the creek bends and you can look down the valley for five miles in either direction, there is a row of teepee rings, the rocks that once held down the edges of buffalo-skin tents now overgrown with pastel cultures of lichen and beginning to sink into the earth. It was an incredibly windy spot to strike camp, but from up there you could watch for game, and see strangers coming for an hour before they arrived. You get a good view of our house, too, a mile away, beaming in all its yellow glory through a tall green veil of poplars that have rooted right down to water.

The house where I grew up was the same house my grandfather'd grown up in, but not really the same house at all. In photographs from his childhood it is a dignified clapboard affair standing boldly on the bald prairie. By the time we moved in, it was completely sheltered in a cove of poplar and Manchurian elms, and in need of major renovations.

My mother chose to have the outside redone in yellow and white aluminum siding, making it look like a double-decker lemon meringue pie.

Our Technicolor house contrasted surreally with the barn across the yard: an immense, brooding, weathered grey structure that looked as if it were about to collapse. I was scared to death of the place—so scared that it gave me bad dreams.

Come to think of it, my first actual un-document-inspired memory might be the nightmare I woke from to the pain of that abscessed tooth—if a dream can properly be called memory. But why not, when it's more vivid to me than what happened yesterday?

(Did anything happen yesterday?)

I was in the barn. I couldn't normally stick my nose into the place without heaving, but now there was no smell. Devils danced in shafts of light that snuck through gaps in the roof. I could see sky through those gaps, slivers of blue, though it must have recently rained because water dripped down into murky puddles on the carpet of manure that hid the cement floor.

Something was watching me.

On one of the rough fir studs that lined the walls I caught a glimpse of a bag spider running for cover behind a woolly tuft of reddish-brown hair wound around a rusty nail. The wind sighed, and the timbers softly moaned.

Then *something* attacked.

I tried to run, but the evil manure grabbed my boots. My hands shot out, trying in vain to save me as I fell forward and plunged into the fetid mess, which pulled me in by all four limbs, leaving me with a simple choice: drown in dung or have my bones torn apart and cracked and sucked for marrow. I decided on the manure, if only for the chance of being reborn from its awful baptism, and prepared to immerse myself, just in time for the light to burn my eyes open to a vision of my mother bending over me saying, "Joan! Enough screaming, Joan!"

Her cool hand on my forehead.

It was the barn, and not the house, that I associated with the grandfather I'd never met. Maybe it was even his spirit that haunted the place in my dreams. The idea of him as a malevolent ghost could easily have arisen from my mother. How many nights did I lie in my pitch-dark bedroom, afraid to go to the bathroom because of monsters under the bed, while downstairs I could hear Mom screaming at Dad about how the "Old Man" had cursed us when he left him "this worthless patch of dirt"?

My grandfather had escaped the farm and built up a paving company into a tiny empire, which still exists and still bears his—and my—last name: *Swift Paving*. Dad grew up in a big house in Regina and worked for the family company a few years before he was enticed back to Broken Head by a government job with the Department of Highways. I suppose he wanted to get out from under the Old Man's thumb, and the Old Man never forgave him, which would explain the curse. The land had been leased for years, bringing in a tidy sum, but the elder Swift must have known his son would be foolish enough to try his hand at running what was, after all, the Swift place.

Mom liked to remind Dad of the inflated land prices when he inherited in the mid-seventies, claiming that if he'd sold we could have lived the rest of our lives off the interest. He'd had a good job when they met, operating one of those machines with the huge roller that flattens asphalt into a surface smooth enough for driving on. A practical skill, but he gave it all up for the dream of being king of his own world. Unfortunately, his timing couldn't have been worse: he borrowed pools of money at high interest to buy all new machinery and by the time the drought of the eighties hit, both the bank and my mother had long since decided his dream was a nightmare.

When I was ten, Brian went off to the barn with his gallon ice cream pail to collect the eggs, only to discover all our chickens had been slaughtered by a weasel. Dad cleaned up the carcasses and threw them on the burnpile before I had a chance to see for myself, but Brian gave me such a graphic description that it almost seems I watched the weasel punching his teeth into those hens' necks and sucking the blood from them. These visions might have led to more nightmares and a stronger claim that I was right to be afraid of the barn, that perhaps I had been seeing through the eyes of a chicken in that dream. But that's not what happened.

Instead, the barn became one of my favourite playgrounds. In its mow Brian and I built straw forts that led off into miles of secret tunnels. It was in one of these forts, by the beam of a flashlight, that Billy Nichol talked me into pulling down my panties so that he could see *mine* and even attempt to prick me with a durum straw before I slapped his hand away.

Sometimes I wonder if we search out our bad dreams and try to inhabit them. Is that why we go to horror movies, ride roller coasters, watch the evening news, drink Southern Comfort mixed with orange juice, desire electric beings who can only inhabit us for a moment before they fade away?

Is that why we fall in love?

After Dad lost the farm and Mom left him, I waitressed at a couple of pizza palaces before I finally landed the job at the library on the strength (I assume, because I didn't have any other related experience) of an impassioned declaration that I'd always loved books. The fellow who was interviewing me—the chairman of the library board at the time, who, to my knowledge, has never borrowed a book from the library—looked slightly embarrassed, as though I'd just confessed to some particularly disgusting form of bestiality. He skimmed my résumé again. "You're a Swift?" he said, and I nodded, and said, "Joan Swift," even though my name was right there at the top of the page he was holding, and he smiled with the cloying self-satisfaction of one who believes he knows more about you than you know about yourself, and he said, "Are you related to Stan?"

"My father." I nodded, and he nodded back.

"I know your father. I used to go fishing along the creek there, at your dad's farm, all the time. How is your dad?"

"He's been better."

"Yes. I hear." He shook his head solemnly. "Too bad. It's a nice spot there along the creek. Great fishing. Great great fishing."

It wasn't a bad job, but the Broken Head Public Library is "hardly the place to seek fame and fortune." At least, that was what Jason told me, before he proved himself wrong.

On the evening of Wednesday, April 23rd, 199–, at 7:15 p.m., Jason Warwick strode into the library wearing a black cashmere overcoat that fell to just above his knees—a costume that in Broken Head only a middle-aged lawyer or banker would have been expected to wear, but this fellow looked like he hadn't yet turned thirty. A camera swayed from a strap around his neck. He walked up to the counter and spoke to me as he peeled off his black leather gloves.

"There's a library board meeting here tonight," he said, not asking but telling me, as if I were the one needing directions—as if he'd just purchased the building and were now considering tearing it down. He did not remove his sunglasses.

"In there." I pointed to the conference room.

He stood inspecting me, so that it became apparent that he hadn't really noticed me until I'd spoken. I thought he was about to speak again, but instead he smiled, nodded, sidled over to the door, glanced back at me, smiled again, and opened the door without knocking. The mayor's voice rose in a string of epithets that made the only mother in the children's section cover her son's ears.

"Who's that?" Susie wanted to know.

"Must be the *Standard*'s new reporter."

"Isn't *he* God's gift to women."

"Seems to think so."

A week later he walked up to the counter again and interrupted me in the middle of a brutal sex slaying—I was hooked on *True Crime* at the time—and, pulling his shades down to the tip of his nose so that I saw his blue eyes for the first time, he introduced himself.

"I'm Jason Warwick. I'm the new reporter at the *Standard*."

You'd have thought he'd said *The Washington Post*. I did my best to make it clear that I knew who he was and I wasn't the least bit impressed with any scribbler who'd had to resort to accepting a job with Broken Head's fifth-rate paper, but he wasn't willing to be put off so easily.

"Listen, we're thinking about starting this new series at the paper—kind of a community column about women in the workplace—and I was wondering if you'd be willing to do an interview with me?"

I could see that he expected me to be honoured.

"You want to interview *me*?"

"Yeah. *You*."

When I didn't respond he placed his hands on the counter, spreading his long, rather pale and feminine fingers in a way that made it seem he was offering them to me. I set my book down, pushing it under the counter so he couldn't see the cover.

"Why me?"

"*Why*? Because *yooou* … are important."

"I am?"

He nodded earnestly. "Libraries are *incredibly* important institutions. When you think about it, the library is the cornerstone of democracy itself, because democracy is meaningless if citizens do not have free and equal access to information; and any citizen, regardless of how rich or poor, regardless of the colour of his or her skin, regardless of what he or she believes, can get any book they want from your shelves, or through your system of interlibrary loans. That kind of a resource is of gigantic importance in small agrarian centres like Broken Head, where access to non-mainstream materials is limited."

I was a little taken aback. Finally, I managed to speak.
"I'm not a library."

He smiled and leaned closer.

"No, but you're the keeper of the books, and I love books."

I couldn't help laughing.

"What's so funny?" he said, finally looking a little offended. That's the way it works with people like Jason: you try to offend them and they don't even notice, and then when you least expect it, you've gone and hurt their feelings.

"That's how I got this job," I explained. "Those were my credentials."

"What were?"

"That I love books. That's what I told the guy at the job interview."

He reached into his overcoat and took out his notebook, making a show of writing this down.

"Cool. Isn't that more important than a piece of paper that says you're a librarian? Sometimes things work better in small towns because people use common sense instead of meaningless bureaucracy." He cocked an eyebrow at me. "Don't you think?"

"Actually ... I got the job because I knew someone." He stopped writing. "*That's* how things work in small towns. Did you get your job because you love newspapers?"

He tapped his pen on the counter.

"You've got a tongue on ya, haven't ya?"

I nodded. "In my mouth."

He stopped tapping.

"I like that. A tongue in her mouth." His tongue appeared between his lips for an instant and then was gone. "I guess I got my job because I write. I worked for a couple of underground publications in Toronto. That's where I'm from: Toronto. I'm also a novelist." I didn't respond, so he seemed to think I hadn't heard him. "I'm writing a novel."

"I keep a diary."

"You write? That's good. I thought you might." He jotted something else in his notebook. "So, what you say?" After one of his effusions Jason would often switch to this kind of verbal shorthand, as if there were an appointment with Boutros Boutros-Ghali he might miss if he wasted the time it took to add a two-letter word like *do*. "Lunch? Tomorrow? Eric's?"

He had this fleck of black in his left iris, which he later explained was caused by a stick in the eye when he was a kid: playing pirates, if I remember correctly. Susie filled me in on the ring on his left hand without me having to ask. She'd discovered through her mother—her mother knew everything that went on in Broken Head—that Jason's wife was Carol MacAndrew, the eldest daughter of Cecil MacAndrew, a local contractor. I didn't know Carol, but did go to school with her younger brother Michael, who'd flown through both his windshield and the back window of the Hutterite van he'd rear-ended in a white-out on the Trans-Canada, and that was the end of him. Carol went to Toronto for a university degree, but wound up married to Jason Warwick instead. They were a family prone to tragedy.

According to what Susie's mother had gleaned from Carol's mother, Jason had moved out of his English professor father's house and into Carol's apartment, but when she lost her job to restructuring she could no longer support him in the fashion he had grown accustomed to, and for some reason his father was unwilling to take him back. Carol's father came to the rescue and fixed up his girl with a job at Universal Realty back in her home town. Jason told his friends he was moving to the country for a while to work on his book.

And so Mr. Jason Warwick woke up one morning and found himself in Broken Head, Saskatchewan. To add insult to injury he found that his own career—which primarily involved going for coffee during the day and going for cocktails during the evening—was in remission, while Carol was suddenly a great success. With the oil and gas boom and all the old farmers within a seventy-five-mile radius selling out and retiring in Broken Head, Universal Realty were experiencing a boom of their own, and, lo and behold, Carol MacAndrew, pretty daughter of a popular local businessman, was their top sales*man*.

"He's not very happy, from what I hear," Susie told me. "City boy. Feels he's out of the hoop."

"It's the loop, Susie: the *loop*." She didn't even bother to look up from her overdue slips. "Doesn't he consider the *Standard* a good career move? Every ladder has a bottom rung."

"Is his wife going along for the date?"

"It's not a *date*. He's interviewing me."

I remember something my mother once told me—or I think I remember. I can't quite recall the context, except that Mom was in the kitchen, down on her hands and knees, scrubbing the black and pink and white tile floor, so it must have been before she had the linoleum put down—years before Dad lost the farm. I can't remember what I said to her, but whatever it was made her toss her rag in her pail of grey suds and sit back to look me in the eye. She said, "Get used to it, Joan: there's never enough love to go around."

What did she mean by that? Was their marriage already in trouble, the end already in sight way back in the time of that pink and black and white tile floor? Was Dad's bankruptcy just an excuse for her to make the escape she'd long been planning? *Excuse* definitely isn't the right word, because it was exactly that interpretation of her leaving that I couldn't excuse: that she'd left Dad because of money. It was what she told me—that she didn't have the strength to support his failures any longer—but remembering her down on her knees that day makes me wonder if it wasn't just a way of explaining what she otherwise couldn't have explained. How do you put love, or the lack of it, into words?

More likely, what she said had nothing to do with Dad. More likely she said it because I'd been whining about some privilege that Brian had had bestowed upon him. I'd probably insisted for the thousandth time that they must love Brian more than me. And Mom, tired of my histrionics, had looked me up and down and said, "Get used to it, Joan: there's never enough love to go around," before she turned her attention back to the dirty pink tile she was working on at that moment.

That's probably how it happened. I really can't remember.

Before we go any further, let's get a few things straight: this is a private confession. I am not casting these pearls before swine, but am offering them as a gift to you, my solitary reader. As you read these words, a great intimacy is happening between *you* and *me*.

Please don't try to deny this.

I know that you will have read and watched other accounts of this sordid affair, all of which have made claims to truth. The difference is that their tellers expected nothing from you, had no respect for you, treated you as just one more willing voyeur peering through a grimy peephole into the bright screen of their imagination.

If you give nothing, then how can you expect to take anything away?

I am imagining you now, reader, settling back in your chair by the fire; or stretching on the couch by the window where you can glance out every now and then at the deer in the garden eating your corn; or making room for someone to sit next to you on the subway (don't allow him to read over your shoulder!); or propped against your pillows in your bed, ignoring the would-be lover next to you who is trying to win your attention away from these words; or behind a locked door, lolling in a pool of bubbles, your knees propped against the enamel on either side of the tub, the book poised above you.

What I am offering you is a relationship. If that's too much of a commitment, then please close these covers. I have no time for Casanovas.

Eric's is a glorified pizza palace owned by the same Greek family who own almost every restaurant in Broken Head, which explains why almost every restaurant in Broken Head has exactly the same menu. It was past the lunch rush, so there weren't many other patrons: just a few local business people sucking down coffee and cigarettes. Jason ordered the ribs and the calamari appetizer, which he offered to share with me.

"No thanks. I never eat anything that might suck back. Haven't you read Jules Verne?"

"*Twenty Thousand Leagues Under the Sea*! My all-time favourite book when I was a kid."

"I never liked those little boys' books."

"Of course not. You were a little girl."

"Never."

The interview started out much as I'd expected—with questions about the library and all of the exigencies of working there—but quickly veered into suspicious territory.

"You're single?"

I left a long enough pause that it was a great wonder such a sensitive man did not squirm.

"No," I finally said. "Today I'm nine people."

And then he did squirm.

"Oh ... I just ... I'm wondering about ... that part of you."

"I have a pretty good idea which *part* of me you're wondering about."

"No, no. What I mean is ... a lot of the young people from around here tend to leave after high school, don't they?"

"I think the UFOs get them."

"Soooooooooo ... what are *you* doing here?"

"I'm from here. Maybe I like it here."

"Okay. Okay. Okay. But don't you find it ... boring?"

"I manage to entertain myself."

"Don't you get lonely? The gene pool's not very deep."

"It's green and it stinks of chlorine? I'm sure I could find as good a man here as anywhere else."

"Really? What do you look for in a man?"

"Blood. Bone. Grey matter."

"The mind's important to you?"

"Not really. Generally I look for those things with a carbide-tipped circular saw."

He set down his pen.

"I guess that explains where all the local youths disappear." He looked away, perhaps imagining the blade whirling. "You're not much of a romantic, are you?"

I twirled my fork as I imagined one might twirl a harpoon, shifting my eyes from the tentacles on his plate to his faintly freckled nose.

"What does this have to do with my job?"

"The story's about you. Do you think of your job as defining you?"

"I don't think anything defines me. What defines you?"

He smiled as though he'd been waiting for me to ask this question, then stretched his arm along the back of his booth, revealing blue veins running along the pale underside of his wrist.

"Nothing. We're an indefinable pair, you and I."

"We are not a pair," I immediately informed him, so that he would not be long misled on this point.

He was silent for a moment, studying me, his expression a bit melancholy, and finally he began to speak. "She dwelt among the untrodden ways beside the springs of Dove, a maid whom there were none to praise and very few to love."

The fluorescent lights created a kind of halo effect on the blond streaks that accented his hundred-dollar haircut. Nobody in Broken Head had given him *that* haircut. I finally managed to stammer, "Is that ... from your novel?"

"No." He was still looking a bit mournful. "That's Wordsworth, not Warwick. You like it?"

"Yeah. It's … nice."

"So you are at least a little romantic, after all?"

"I like words. They're … useful. Is there more?"

"Pardon? More words?"

"Yeah? Is there more to the poem?"

"Oh, you don't want to hear it. She dies in the end."

"Don't we all?"

He laughed a nervous laugh.

"Let me see. 'A violet by a mossy stone half hidden from the eye. Fair as a star, when only one is shining in the sky. She lived unknown, and few could know when Lucy ceased to be; but she is in her grave, and, oh, the difference to me.'"

He picked up a tentacle, then thought better of it, and set it back on the plate.

"Why did you memorize that?"

"Oh, my father's always reciting poetry, and if you hear it enough times, some of it's bound to stick."

"You have a father who recites poetry."

"Yeah. He wrote a book about Byron's relationship with bears. You probably haven't read it. As far as I know, there isn't anyone who's read it."

"I like Blake."

"Really? Recite something."

"Oh, I don't know: 'Tiger Tiger, burning bright, all the way from morn till night.' I don't remember."

He grinned, the mark of that sword fight floating there next to his iris.

"'Did he smile his work to see? Did he who made the Lamb make thee?'" Perhaps expecting an answer, he let the question hang, and when I offered none he said, "The

Romantics were all for following their instincts. You ever just follow your instincts?"

I swallowed and shifted against the sticky vinyl. Something strange was happening: his thoughts were becoming so obvious, so palpably present in his eyes, that they were beginning to slip inside my skull and I was imagining him imagining his lips on my breasts.

"Sure. It's a good recipe for disaster."

"You think so? Is it better to go around regretting for the rest of your life what you didn't do, but wish you had done?"

"It's better than going around regretting what you *did* do."

"I don't think so."

"So you believe that you should just follow your nose like a dog into whatever cranny it happens to lead you to?"

"I wouldn't have put it quite that way."

"How would you have put it?"

He leaned closer, his tie falling into what was left of his baked potato.

"I feel like I know you. It's like … you were already inside my head before I saw you behind the library counter. Sitting on that stool. Your eyes burning holes in that book. Your back … so perfectly straight. I feel like it's no accident we met."

"Really? And what about your wife? Did you meet her by accident?"

That backed him off, settling him against the cushions behind him. I smiled sweetly, hoping that he would glimpse the threat of chaos in my white teeth. He sighed, casting his unholy blue eyes up at Eric's speckled ceiling.

"What about my *wife*?"

"Oh, I'm just curious. Is she some sort of masochist? Or does she just have bad taste?"

He was still looking at the ceiling.

"It's a long story."

I crossed my arms.

"I'm all ears."

He thought it over, then looked down from the ceiling and glanced around the room, checking to see if we were safe from eavesdroppers in the adjacent booths.

"Okay," he said, and then, leaning in a few inches from my nose, "I apologize."

That was it. Then he just sat there staring at me from far too close, waiting for a response.

"That's the shortest long story I've ever heard."

"No. You're right. I guess I'm pretty transparent." He stared into his hands, and he was actually blushing. "I concocted this whole interview thing just to get a chance to talk to you. It was a dumb idea. I mean, I really did want to interview you because I could tell right away that you're ... different. But I should have been more up front."

"I thought you were going to tell me about your wife?"

He looked up at the ceiling again, blinking rapidly, either slightly embarrassed or telling this to someone up there in the sky. "I don't have a wife. We wear rings for business reasons. What might clients think about their real estate agent dwelling in sin? This is the Bible belt, you know."

"Soooo, you have a purely professional relationship?"

"Carol and I? She's got her life, I've got mine. That's all really beside the point. I'm apologizing for my behaviour, for not being more straight up with you. I'm not apologizing for my relationship. Carol and I want different things." He looked directly at me and shrugged in a way that made me feel very much a small-town girl. I wanted to tell him to stop, that it was none of my business, but I couldn't open my mouth, so he just ploughed on, peering awkwardly into his hands, reading his own palms. "She wants Broken Head, I want Toronto. She wants Cheddar, I want Gruyère. She wants … She thinks she wants kids some day, but she's too busy with her career for the moment."

Over his right shoulder, in a booth across the room, I could see Don Hiller, a business associate of Carol's father, having coffee and discussing the weather.

"And you want kids *now*?" I heard myself asking.

"No. There's already too many unwanted children on this planet. I was an accident. Not a happy accident. I wouldn't want to create another me, would I?" He smiled sheepishly. "Anyway, what do you care. I apologize for being such an awful boor. It's just that … you're very beautiful."

He left it there, waiting for me to respond. The room spun around the axis of my brain. His right hand dropped from the table, where it had been resting, and disappeared. I waited, but the touch never came. I put my hand over my mouth, trying to think of something to say, wondering if I should simply stand and walk away without speaking another word. Graciously, he helped me to escape.

"Finish your coffee. Tell me *your* tragedies."

My mother liked to tell a story about how she'd met my father at a dance: how she'd spotted him watching her as he slouched against the wall near the door, obviously prepared for a quick escape, and how he'd been too shy to ask her for a dance so she had finally walked up to him and asked him herself, even though that wasn't the way things were done back then.

Dad insisted that this had never happened. He had met her at a wedding. One of her friends was marrying one of Dad's cousins. When he saw her he asked his auntie who she was and when his auntie told him that Mom attended church every week my father took a sudden interest in religious matters.

"Well, that may be," my mother said. "But I met *you* at the wedding dance that night."

"I've told you a thousand times, I never went to that dance," my father said. "It must have been some other young slob you were gyrating with."

"It was not. It was you. And I've still got the bruises on my feet to prove it."

"I've never been to a wedding dance in my life."

"He maintains this," Mother said, turning to my brother Brian, "because he's so proud that he got too drunk to come to his own."

"I had every intention of coming"—Dad turned to me—"but *she* wouldn't let me."

At which point mother would get up and huff away from the table, leaving Dad to give us a wink and say, "She was wearing a blue dress at that dance, and I'll tell ya, blue has never looked so good."

I believe in love at first sight.

Not that I'm romantic. On the contrary, I believe that love is not destiny, but body chemistry. You meet someone, and almost immediately—even before you know it—you know that you want to spend all your time with him, that you want to breathe the smell of him inside you, that you want to run your hands and your lips down his back, bury your nose in his chest. And he looks at you, and he knows that about you, and he wants almost the same things from you: the birthmark beside your belly button, your breasts, the curve of your hip under his hand, his lips on your thighs, the smell of you inside him.

Not that I'm saying it's entirely physical. I'm not talking about lust, after all. What divides it from lust is the eyes. You want inside his eyes, and he wants inside yours, and you both know it in your gut before you know it in your brain—you feel it curled there like something has taken root and begun to grow. You also feel it in your arms, your lower back, your neck. It's a tingling sensation, as though you're suddenly aware of the blood moving in your veins.

You could back away. You can deny the gut, but it's not easy, because the gut makes the brain do funny things. And if you'd prefer not to resist, you can always blame it on bad luck. Or bad dreams.

I figured I'd used up my fifteen minutes of fame when Jason's article came out in the *Standard*. For a week I ran into myself everywhere I went: posed on the front page, smiling unnaturally, pushing a book into place on a shelf. Susie was mournfully jealous, wishing that it had been her face endlessly repeated on all that paper, and so I tried to belittle the whole experience as an embarrassment, which only made her more remote. Half a dozen of my mother's friends called to tell me how much they'd enjoyed the article. Library circulation jumped by three per cent.

The place was hopping the evening Jason's call came, though that likely had more to do with high school exams than my phony smile. I stamped the twenty-third Harlequin for a young mother and left a teenager waiting with his *Gun Digest* while I answered the tenth ring.

"Joan, it's Jason Warwick. I need to see you right away."

"Pardon?"

"I need to see you right now. Can you get away?"

The teenager at the counter shoved his finger up his nose to the middle joint. "My brain's itchy," he said.

"I'm kinda busy right now," I whispered into the receiver.

"Write down this address: 453 Washburn Crescent. It's on the south side."

"I know …"

"I'll meet you there."

Click.

I told Susie that there'd been a family emergency and left her to deal with the crush.

As it turned out, I knew the house very well. It was Laurie Johnson's house. On Laurie's tenth birthday, about a decade before, I'd stayed there for a sleepover. We got into a pillow fight in the middle of the night and Laurie was yanked upstairs to her bedroom, leaving the rest of us to plot the demise of her parents. Breakfast was a solemn affair.

Feeling more than a bit self-conscious, more than a bit vulnerable, I walked up to the door and pressed the bell. Jason opened it immediately and frantically motioned me inside. I stepped over the threshold and looked around, trying to get my bearings. Laurie's grad photo smiled at me from its place of honour on the television.

"What's up?"

"I need to talk to you."

"What are we doing here?"

He looked around as if it were just dawning on him that he was in someone else's home.

"It's one of Carol's. They're asking eighty-five." His eyes returned to me. "They're dreaming."

For an instant I wondered if he was intending to try to sell me Laurie Johnson's parents' home.

"I can't stop thinking about you," he said. "I have this image of your eyes—of you looking at me the way you are right now, and I can't get it out of my brain."

The expression on his face reminded me of the Border collie we'd had on the farm—Nero was his name—after he'd pissed on the floor. I was speechless. Almost.

"Have you tried drugs?"

"We have to talk," he said, and he grabbed my hand and led me into the hallway, where they couldn't see us from the street, and instead of talking he started kissing me, and, lo and behold, I found myself accepting and returning that kiss, and he began to unbutton my blouse, then continued undressing me until I was completely naked and he was crouched before me kissing me in a way that was so much like my most preposterous fantasies I had trouble believing it was actually happening. What made it almost real was that it was not nearly as deliciously pleasurable as it had been in the imaginary world of those fantasies: I was too much aware of my own nakedness, the pebbled wall against my back, the Johnson family photos staring at me from across the hall. All the same, I allowed him to continue. Finally, he stood and led me on down the hallway to Mr. and Mrs. Johnson's bedroom.

Afterwards, he turned on the news.

There I was, in Mr. and Mrs. Johnson's bed, my sweat and various other bodily fluids on Mr. and Mrs. Johnson's sheets, and he was watching Peter Mansbridge recite the day's events. There was some story that he just had to see—a demonstration in front of the U.S. Consulate in Toronto that an acquaintance was reporting on. Though the acquaintance was supposedly a friend, he savagely mimicked the fellow's self-important delivery. I suppose he thought I'd be impressed, and to be painfully honest, I suppose I was. He went on about the private absurdities behind those images and that voice but he didn't succeed in making them seem mundane. Instead, it was as though he had entered the screen himself; he really was one of them, one of the exotics from the other side.

Yes, young Joan was smitten.

But mostly I just wanted to get out of there. I kept imagining Carol walking in with a couple of prospective buyers. Or Mr. and Mrs. Johnson. Apparently they were on Vancouver Island scouting out a new home, but this was still their house, and they could return to it any time they wanted. He sat propped against their headboard, making snide comments about the metaphors used by reporters in Rwanda or Yugoslavia and when I asked him why it mattered—what difference it made if the Serbian mortars were described as a battering ram in the same sentence that the Serbs had been described as a massive wave—he told me that "the moral and ethical standards of any society can be seen reflected in the stories that society chooses to tell and in the way the tellers tell those stories. Sloppy writing reflects sloppy thinking and sloppy thinking leads to sloppy morals."

He reeled all of this off without averting his gaze from the television. I pinched a hair on his chest between my fingertips and yanked it out. He flinched, and for a moment his eyes were not trained on the picture tube.

"As far as I can see a mortar hole through the wall makes any words seem pretty inadequate."

He sighed.

"If I could have that asshole's job in Yugoslavia I'd leave tomorrow."

And I believed him.

Now I think that he really didn't feel he deserved to go— didn't deserve to scramble through crumbling buildings looking for cover from snipers' shells—didn't deserve to have a gun pointed at his head and be told to kiss the ground. Deep down inside he felt he *deserved* to sit in Broken Head city council meetings, listening to the mayor hand out favours to his buddies but writing about the parking meter debate because that was the only story he could get by his editor.

But at that moment, in that bed, I believed in his brave ambitions. He was destined for the real world, and I was only a brief stop along his way.

A wave of self-consciousness overcame me. It was clear to me that having had me, he knew that I was not really what he wanted, and that I might as well leave with as much dignity as I could marshal before any further disaster occurred. I threw off the Johnsons' down comforter and climbed out of bed with the intention of getting dressed and walking out of Jason Warwick's life forever, before realizing that I'd have to fetch all of my clothes from the hallway. For the moment, at least, Jason had turned away from Mansbridge to look at me.

"Doesn't any news happen here?" I asked him.

He stared at my breasts.

"Goodwin," he said. "Nothing except Goodwin."

T he untimely, tragic, and meaningless death of Goodwin's father must have been the catalyst for his absurd (under the circumstances) and tragic inner yearning for greatness. Goodwin did not wish to share his father's destiny: to drown that way, in his own thankless harvest, and leave nothing for the world to remember. There must have been a part of his desire for Stephanie Rush that was a manifestation of his longing to cheat his own ignoble fate by joining the ranks of those who have three names: Jean-Jacques Rousseau, William Butler Yeats, Pierre Elliott Trudeau, Jennifer Jason Leigh.

John Wilkes Booth. Lee Harvey Oswald. Darwin Andrew Goodwin. They always have three names, a practice meant to distinguish them from all the innocent Lee Oswalds and Darwin Goodwins in the world, and it also had the effect of frustrating Goodwin's rather pitiful attempts to hide from his reputation by calling himself by his middle name.

He had been convicted of lunacy, and his sentence was fame.

Yes, Darwin Andrew Goodwin succeeded in becoming Broken Head's most famous citizen. He was an ongoing human interest story. He was a clown in the media circus that celebrated the end of the Second Millennium. His face graced the front page of The National Enquirer *and* The New York Times. *Before his sensational recent arrest, he had already been jailed more than half a dozen times for violating injunctions requiring that he not contact Stephanie Rush. He was once apprehended trying to break into her mansion in Malibu and had been turned back at the U.S. border any number of times. His condition has been written about by countless psychiatrists and is categorized as* erotic obsessive *or* erotomania. *In short, he is one of North America's most famous lunatics. And the television, newspaper and magazine stories always contained the line "Goodwin lives near Broken Head, Saskatchewan." It was the kind of notoriety that made even the Broken Head Chamber of Commerce uncomfortable.*

Perhaps they should have thanked him. If it were not for Goodwin, no one would have heard of Broken Head. The name of the town is a translation of the Indian name for an American whisky trader's station that was located in that valley for one winter before there was anything else; apparently the name derives from the fact that a patron fell off his horse and split open his skull after sampling some of the trader's wares.

Broken Head is not as small as one might imagine—not two streets and a grain elevator. The boosters of the community long ago claimed the status of city, though what that word means on the Canadian Prairies is not quite what it means in the rest of the world. More people go to the average National Hockey League game than live in Broken Head.

The common characteristic that unites the citizens of Broken Head is a desire to be somewhere else; in other words, what links the community is a tendency toward dissolution. The best lack all conviction, while the worst are wintering in Arizona.

It's understandable: they'd rather be somewhere warmer. Somewhere richer. Some place that gets on television more often. They have that same fantasy of fame that Goodwin had, and some of them even pitifully attempt to imitate the famous places and people they see on television—wearing their knockoffs, carrying their cell phones—hoping to make themselves feel alive and attached to the real world going on out there that they watch on their screens. On the other hand, they can't help but be vaguely aware that they are living in a quaint parody of a world that no longer exists, while reality insists that to survive they must move to the city. There's no longer any economic justification for all of those little farms: a few large industrial operations could do the job more efficiently. And as they flee the land there's no one left to support the businesses in the little towns all around them. Broken Head fights the tide by sucking in the retiring farmers, but that can't go on forever. The population is aging, the schools closing. Any moment their world will flicker and disappear. Every few months another store or restaurant *closes. Nobody shops on Main Street any more. There's two malls off the northern edge of town. Things were bad downtown when there was just the one mall. Only God and the developer's friends on council know why they built the second one.*

The community's collective inferiority complex manifests itself most clearly in their city fathers, who try to stem the bleeding by claiming that they're every bit as good as any other place and they're on the verge of making themselves much better—just you wait and see. And so they wait and wait, applauding the addition of each new fast food restaurant on the Trans-Canada service road ("shows the faith this international franchise has in our community" the editor of The Broken Head Standard *tells them) as though they were all Grand Opera Houses, with the result that they can never begin to content themselves with living where they would find the soles of their shoes meeting the ground if they were ever to look down.*

But even if they did look down, all they would see is that bleak brown prairie. So instead they turn on their televisions and their computers, surfing for some glimpse of themselves, but only ever finding one brief image that has any reference to them at all: the paranoid eyes of Darwin Andrew Goodwin.

An excerpt from
Make Believe Love
By Jason Warwick

[Sunday, June 11th]

Day 2. Worked until the wee hours, so I'm
a bit late getting going here. Dad's already
been to church and picked up yesterday's paper from the
drug store so that we can keep up with what a few writers
in Southern Ontario are obsessing about at the moment.

I see that *Make Believe Love*, Jason's unauthorized bio
of Goodwin, has disappeared altogether from the best-
seller list. It never managed to climb above *nine*. Not
exactly the success Jason was counting on. The book by the
American writer, which focuses almost entirely on
Stephanie Rush, was just too much competition. Jason's
book *has* done well in Broken Head, of course. The waiting
list at the library is over an inch thick, Mom told me,
despite the fact that they own five copies. It's the kind of
book Jason despises, but from the start he saw it as a necessary compromise: the money he earned from it would
allow him to buy the time to write his masterpiece.

It has to be a terrible disappointment for him: he was hoping for Oprah and instead he gets Valerie Pringle calling him by the wrong name. Right in the middle of the interview she suddenly starts calling him Bruce. And he makes the mistake of correcting her. It was one of those moments that makes you fidget with your remote, a little embarrassed for them both, but somehow unable to switch the channel.

I'm sure that ever since he was a child Jason has longed for the kind of unconditional love that only Oprah can provide. He wants everyone to love him. The whole world. Not that he thinks he deserves all that love. But that only makes him want it more. He hated Carol for dragging him to this backwater town where it seemed impossible that anybody out there in the real world would ever hear of him. But he didn't give up. He believed that even in Broken Head things could happen that people out there would want to hear about.

For instance, works of art could be destroyed.

The painting was crap. It was a silkscreen, actually, as Ivan, the director of the gallery, explained to me: part of the University of Lethbridge's impressive American print collection. I don't know enough about art to appreciate the difference. To me, it looked like a cheap poster, and Ivan said it was one of 10,000 copies, which made all the hoopla about the destruction of an irreplaceable object seem all the more ridiculous, but Ivan insisted that the glitter applied to her nipples made her one-of-a-kind. The thing's value—priceless, according to Jason's story in the *Standard*; $15,000, so far as the insurance company were concerned—had nothing to do with the picture and everything to do with the name scrawled at the bottom: *Andy Warhol*. Maybe it had something to do with those famous breasts as well, but anybody who'd pay $15,000 for a shot of Stephanie Rush's mammaries ought to have a look at the overpass in Broken Head. I could make him a real deal.

But what do I know about art, you're asking?

Well, let me see. I know this:

One lovely June morning much like the one outside my window, but years ago, when I was fifteen, I was lounging in our tiny bathtub in our rusty-smelling and yellowish, unfluoridated farm well water, listening to a riot of birds in the trees outside that open window, when the door flew open and my thirteen-year-old brother burst in with my mother's video camera already recording. I *had* locked the door, but all of the bedroom doors and the bathroom door could be easily picked with a bobby pin or a curtain hook.

The problem was, I'd descended so far into the trance a hot bath can bring on that I didn't hear him picking the lock and was unable to get to the towels first, so all I could do was curl my body into a fetal ball meant to protect all of my private places from the lens, and scream threats of what I would do to him once I got my hands on him. No one else was home, unfortunately, so he simply stood there and continued to film, trying for different angles that might reveal a glimpse of what I was trying so desperately to hide, and when I changed my tactics and attempted to grab for him or the camera, I only succeeded in leaving myself exposed. I briefly tried negotiating to get him to leave, offering him his life if he agreed to put down the camera, leave me the videotape, and walk out of the room. He just giggled. I tried begging, assuring him that if he left me the tape I would not tell Mom and Dad, which would mean he could escape this little mistake of his without any great consequences. He giggled some more.

And finally, I snapped.

"You want to see them? You want to see my tits? You want to see my cunt?"

I rose to my feet, giving him a full frontal shot, then lunged at him, but I slipped and tumbled face first on the pink terry bathmat. Brian, I saw later, continued to film. The indignity far surpassed the pain, as I'd managed to break my fall with my arms, but I instantly decided that the best thing to do was take advantage of the accident and pretend that I had been knocked cold or killed. It turned out to be the perfect plan. As you watch the film, Brian begins to nervously call my name, then actually reaches his stockinged foot into the frame to jostle my head, hoping that will rouse me. When it doesn't, he panics, turns, and runs.

I'm not sure what he did while he was gone. He didn't call an ambulance. Perhaps he was looking for a good place to bury me. At any rate, when he returned to the scene a few minutes later I ambushed him and got the camera, which he was still holding. There wasn't much fight in him. He was too chastened by circumstances, and relieved that I wasn't dead, to want to hold on to any evidence of his crime.

The tape is hidden in a safe place. I'd planned to record over it, but after watching it I couldn't. There's something about the look in my eye as I rise up to face him, and there is something in my lunge and my fall, and there is something in my naked back as I lie there dead or dying, that I simply could not wipe away.

It's easily more of a work of art than Warhol's silly picture.

—⊙

Brian, my gifted little brother, eventually gave up art and escaped to university in Saskatoon to study engineering, and though Dad offered to hire him to work on the farm, he found a summer job as an assistant meat-cutter in a grocery store. And so Dad hired me to cook and clean and do odd chores that required an extra pair of hands. "Better than giving the money to the bank."

Mom was absolutely furious. "Why would you want to live out there?" She had recently moved to town and bought a condominium with her half of the marriage settlement. How she managed this still mystifies me, as that fall the bank took the farm completely, and I wonder how half of a quarter-million in the hole can be any more than nothing. Math was never one of Dad's strong points.

"My whole life I listened to you whining, 'Can I go to town. I need a ride to town. Who's gonna take me to town!' and now, no sooner do I *move* you to town and give you your own room with your own *bath*room, and you want to move back to the farm and clean your father's toilet."

Clean it for money. And the best thing was that Dad didn't interfere with what I did on my own time. I was going out with Melvin Campbell who was in grade eleven and had been given a Toyota Celica for his sixteenth birthday, so there was no problem getting to town when I wanted. And every weekend a bunch of us partied in our pasture, down by the creek, where we'd build a campfire and listen to music from the car stereo and drink beer and smoke pot and skinny-dip and sleep right there on the ground, looking up into a crowd of stars.

Dad never bothered us. He had his own parties, quietly working his way through bottle after bottle of rye, no matter what night of the week it happened to be, while he watched whatever happened to be on television. His silent brooding was a welcome relief from the operatic screaming sessions I'd lived with for as long as I could remember.

When I started grade twelve in the fall, I stayed on the farm, riding the bus to school, just as I always had. Often Melvin would drive me home and I would make supper for him and Dad. I told myself that life was fine. If my mother didn't love my father, had only married him because of an accident that turned out to be *me*, that was okay. It didn't mean *I* had to be unhappy. I had found true love, and Melvin and I would be together forever.

By November it had started to snow and the bank had foreclosed and Melvin had decided that he needed some space. I told him I wasn't sure I could kick him that high. Dad moved into a couple of rooms above an insurance place on First West, and there wasn't much choice for me but to move back in with my mother.

"Didn't I tell you?" she said over and over again, in reference to virtually everything that had ever occurred.

I only stayed as long as I had to. The waitressing jobs didn't pay enough to scrape together rent—almost nobody tips in Broken Head—but the summer after I graduated I got on at the library, and not long after that I approached my new friend Susie, who did the overdues, with the idea of sharing the rent on a house. So we rounded up some scruffy furniture from garage sales and the Sally Ann and went out on our own.

The small house we rented was in the oldest part of town, about a block from where the creek snaked its way into

Wassimo Park, not far from where the old steam locomotives would have taken on water, which, when it came right down to it—because the trading post that gave Broken Head its name was long gone when the railroad went through—was the biggest reason Broken Head existed at all. The houses on either side of us were empty, with greying siding, broken or boarded-over windows, and jungles of dandelions for lawns. Our neighbours were ghosts. Susie claimed to have met one as she was coming home from the library one evening: an old woman digging in the front yard who said to her, "And how are you this lovely morning?" Susie ran into our house and hid in the closet. I assured her that the woman was only an escapee from the old folks' home, but Susie never walked by that house again without speeding up a couple of klicks.

Ours was what is known as a character home. All of the walls were done in faux pine wallboard that had bowed from moisture. The landlord had dealt with this problem by taping the seams together with shiny duct-tape. There was only the one bedroom, so I slept in the living room on an orange floral pull-out couch that Susie's parents donated from their rumpus room. Sometimes it was hell not having an inch of private space, but I'd proposed the idea myself when Susie insisted on turning down the house because there was only one bedroom. Actually, she'd suggested that we share the tiny bedroom, but that idea didn't appeal to me, so I'd countered with a plan to split the bedroom, each of us getting it for a month at a time, but there was no way she'd agree to sleep in the living room. It wasn't out of any greed on her part; it was fear. I was in the living room so that I could guard us from any barbarians who happened by and decided to break down the door.

Despite the fact that her parents were always encouraging her to go off to university, Susie had not abandoned Broken Head after she finished high school. She wasn't a model of self-confidence and I suppose that when she looked out and saw her entire life waiting for her, staying home to live with Mom and Dad seemed like a safer course than jumping into the abyss. She was five years older than me, but there was something so completely innocent about her that she seemed more like a little sister. I suspect she was a virgin. She claimed to have had a boyfriend for a couple of years, a young scientist who had come to work at the Agricultural Research Station and then had moved on when his contract ran out, but there was something so vague about this fellow, so lacking in detail—so Harlequinesque—that I think she might have made him up. Certainly her story of her first time, which took place in the bedroom of a local boy who had gone on to become an MD and had returned to practise in Broken Head (and was now her doctor), sounded suspiciously like a romance-novel fantasy. Susie could not supply a convincing or consistent account of how they had come to be together in that bedroom and, try as I might, I couldn't manage to picture them there. But then, who knows? sometimes life is even bigger than my imagination.

And so we went out on our own. Bought our own groceries, made our own meals, got dressed up on Friday nights and went for drinks at the sports bar where our contemporaries hung out, or the hotel bar, where the cowboys came to drink their rye-and-Cokes and do the box step.

They were good times. Hard to believe it wasn't that long ago. Before Jason.

"There's the most famous man in Broken Head," Susie whispered in my ear one day, not long after we'd moved in together. We were at work. She was pointing at the guy using the photocopier.

"What?"

My voice was too loud and he turned around. Susie and I looked away. Neither of us could think of anything to say, so we posed dumbly while he scrutinized our backs. When he returned his attention to his reproducing, Susie pulled me into the office where we could watch him between the posters taped over the window.

"You know who he is, eh?"

"The most famous man in town?"

She nodded. The look of sincerity in her eyes could have made me believe in angels, so I took another peek at the man standing in front of the photocopier. There was no sign that he was aware of us now; he seemed hypnotized by the sight of paper spitting from the machine. He was a farmer, judging by the greasy orange cap, the stubble on his face, the beige workpants, the leather workboots with globs of dried green manure showing on the edges of his soles.

"Suuuure he is."

"I'm not kidding!" Susie insisted.

He was about forty-five years old, about five nine, and carrying about twenty excess pounds around his waist.

"He doesn't look like he plays hockey," I said, only partly as a joke, because I thought maybe he could have been a retired professional hockey player. Just about all the famous people from around Broken Head are hockey players, but so far as I know none of them live here any more.

"Noooo," Susie pinched my arm, an annoying habit of hers. "I mean really famous. This guy's been on 'Entertainment Tonight.'"

"'Entertainment Tonight?'"

"Yes," Susie giggled.

I changed tactics, hoping she'd accidentally tell me who he was if I started pointing out the hiccups in her story.

"Wayne Gretzky's been on 'Entertainment Tonight.'"

"That's not Wayne Gretzky."

"Noooo? Well, is it his wife then—Jane—or whatever her name is?"

Susie always ignored my sarcasm, which was possibly the biggest reason why we got along so well.

"This guy is almost as famous as Wayne Gretzky."

"If he's so famous, how come I don't recognize him?"

"You've heard of him. You've seen his picture in the papers."

I looked at him again, but the jowly profile wasn't familiar. All I could come up with was the head of the local chapter of the National Farmers' Union, and I doubted *he'd* ever been on "Entertainment Tonight."

"Oh, come on, Susie. Wayne Gretzky does Coke ads. This guy doesn't look like he's gonna throw much of a scare into Pepsi."

Susie smiled all the more serenely. "Wayne Gretzky's never had a Broadway play written about him."

"That guy's had a Broadway play written about him?"

"Yesss," Susie hissed, like a snake selling apples, then stood there grinning that infuriating grin of hers.

"Oh, now I recognize him. I can't believe it. It's Jean Valjean. Who'd have thought it? Jean Valjean, and he's right here in our little old library in little old Broken Head. I feel less miserable already."

Susie had dragged me all the way to Regina to see *Les Miz*. She was always gushing about what a beautiful Adonis the actor who played dear Jean was. "Tell you the truth, I don't know what you see in him, Susie. He looks to me like he's stolen a few too many loaves. They must've let him eat cake or something …"

She bent over her interlibrary loans, ignoring me.

"Okay, I give up. Who is he?"

I didn't really expect her to tell me: Susie is anything but merciful.

"You have to guess," she said.

It was her favourite game, and if ever I made the mistake of asking her anything—like what spices she'd used in the spaghetti or what disc she'd just put on the stereo, or what was the name of the new perfume she was wearing, or who had tried hitting on her at the mall—she'd always make me guess; and even though it drove me crazy, I always did, which was the other major reason we got along so well.

So I started trying to think of all the famous people in Broken Head, and the first person who came to mind was the mayor, because I'd just finished clipping out a story about him from the Regina paper not twenty minutes before. It was about the shares he owned in a company that got a few monetary favours from the City—tax breaks, et cetera. Of course, he denied that there was anything underhanded going on, said the scandal was dreamed up by those Regina media hacks, and who would doubt him? Not his pal, the editor of the *Standard*, who had written an editorial defending the mayor.

But anyway, the man using the photocopier wasn't the mayor.

"Entertainment Tonight" was a good clue. I racked my brain for a famous entertainer who lived around here. There was a local girl who sang in the Billy Graham choir. Could this be her father? I began to imagine how it might have come about—how they'd done a story about the Billy Graham choir on "Entertainment Tonight" and her father happened to be visiting her at the time and was lucky enough to get his face in the way of the camera for five seconds. But somehow this didn't seem like much of a basis for a Broadway musical.

A regular approached the counter—a mousy little woman who clerked at the EasyMart—and checked out *How to Be Your Own Best Friend* and *Healing Your Aloneness*.

So who else was famous? There was the guy who did the reports from Eastern Europe on the late-night news. Every time he came on Susie'd say, "He's from Broken Head, you know?" and I always knew. Everyone in town knew. The idea of a reporter originating in Broken Head and ending up in Moscow infuriated Jason, who was constantly being told that maybe some day he'd be just as famous as … that guy on the news who was born in Broken Head. I'd never actually met anyone who knew the intrepid reporter when he lived here, which led to my theory (Jason liked my theory and Susie didn't) about how he was born prematurely, in the back of a Volkswagen, while his parents were on their way through town, en route to Winnipeg or Warsaw. The reporter always looked like he was in a hurry.

But excuse the digression. As I said earlier, this all happened Before Jason.

Try as I might, I could not come up with any more media magnets from Broken Head. Except for the odd hockey player, and we'd already ruled them out.

Whoever our friend was, he had a lot of photocopying to do. I started emptying the book return bin and was finished by the time he pulled the key out, brought it to the counter, and handed it to me. His eyes were beer-bottle brown and kind of nasty when combined with the way his lips twisted, but not really threatening because he didn't seem to be looking at me, even though he was. I mean, he was looking at me, but he might as well have been looking at a surveillance camera.

He'd made seventy-nine copies, all on legal-sized paper.

"That'll be $15.80," I said without pausing to think about it for more than a second. The library didn't even have a calculator, forcing us to work out charges longhand, so my incredible talent with numbers usually impressed people. He threw down a twenty and I gave him the change.

"Can I have a receipt for that?"

He looked over my shoulder, asking the wall behind me. I couldn't help but smile. He must have noticed. In his eyes I could see for the first time that he was seeing me.

"Who should I make it out to?"

I stared at the paper, the pen poised there at the line where I would write his name, but the long pause made it seem he was thinking twice about answering. And then, at last, he spoke.

"Joan?"

I looked up. "Pardon?"

His face had transformed: that malignant curl was gone from his lips, and his eyes had softened into something approaching rosewood. He might have been handsome, I realized. Once, long ago, someone could have loved this man.

"Aren't you Joan Swift? Little Joan Swift all grown up?"

I managed to nod my head. "Y ... yeeah? You are?"

"Andy Goodwin. Well, isn't that somethin'. Little Joanie Swift. Beautiful little girl. Knew her when she was only this high." He held out his hand at belt level to show me. "Just about the prettiest little girl in the world. How's your dad doing these days? Sold the farm, didn't he?"

"Yeah." I wrote his name and filled in the figures without glancing up at him again, then ripped out the page and offered it to him.

"Isn't that something. That is really something," he said, stuffing the receipt into his wallet. "Just as cute as you ever was. Say hello to your dad."

"I ... will."

"See you around, then."

He had this awkward grin on his face, so unwieldy it looked as though it might slide off and land on the counter between us. I began straightening up the pamphlets and bookmarks. Finally he turned and left.

"Oh my God, he's in love with you! Creepy! Phone the cops."

"What are you talking about?"

"You know who he is, don't you?"

"What would I tell the cops? That some guy said I was pretty?"

"He ..."

"*Broad*way musical."

"There was!"

"Like hell."

"There was! I heard it on the radio. Somebody wrote a play about Stephanie Rush and him, and Stephanie Rush sued the guy."

"Yeah, I heard about it. Is Winnipeg on Broadway now? They're gonna have to do something about that continental drift."

"Was it in Winnipeg? Well, it was a play."

She seemed to think that all plays must sooner or later end up on Broadway, just as all rocks must sooner or later work their way to the surface of the earth. Ask any farmer.

"Darwin Goodwin," I said, shaking my head.

"Darwin *Andy* Goodwin! You know him! He knows *you!*"

I shrugged. "He was our neighbour."

"How come you didn't recognize him?"

"I haven't seen him since I was—I don't know, five years old? He used to help my dad fix his machinery, but Mom didn't want him on our property and he finally took the hint and stopped coming. He lived just two miles away, but I never saw him. He planted all these trees. You couldn't see anything from the road because of all the trees."

"He's in the paper! He's on the news!"

"Yeah, but he doesn't look like his pictures. Did you think he looks like his pictures?"

"Of course he looks like his picture. How can you not look like your picture?"

"I don't know: his pictures look like some crazy guy. He just looks like any old farmer."

"Darwin Andy Goodwin." Susie shook her head. "And he's in love with you. What if he starts following you? Aren't you scared?"

Maybe I was a little worried, but I wasn't about to admit that to Susie.

Dad was coming over for supper that evening. I invited him as often as I could because he and Susie seemed to get along fine—if she was a little sister to me, she was just as much a sweet obedient daughter to Dad—and I knew he didn't eat properly if he had to cook for himself. It was a skill he'd never acquired, as though he had been passed without transition from his own mother to mine. He hadn't, but there'd probably been a lot of restaurants and TV dinners to fill the gap.

I was at the stove, stirring a bubbling pot of tomato sauce, when he walked in the door and Susie sprang the news of Darwin Andrew Goodwin.

"Oh, yeah. Always seemed to show up for a visit when your mom wasn't around. He knew she didn't like him. I'd make him a cup of tea and he'd pick up Joanie and bounce her on his knee."

"Me? On his knee?"

"Yeah?" Dad said.

Susie eyed me with that expression she usually reserved for when she needed me to rescue the bathtub from a spider.

"And you'd let him?"

"Whaddaya mean, let him? All he was doing was bouncin' ya."

There was enough defensiveness in his answer that it was obvious mom had asked him the same question a thousand times. He picked up one of Susie's knick-knacks off the counter (a porcelain penguin: Susie thought it was a

good idea to collect something, and she'd chosen penguins)
and examined it carefully.

"He hasn't got himself into trouble in years. I don't
know why people can't just leave the poor guy alone."

We both took this to mean *us* and let the subject drop.

Dad set to work sanding down our back door, a job
he'd taken it upon himself to do when he saw "there was
good wood under that green paint," and despite the fact
that I'd told him more than once that I was satisfied with
a green door.

Once I'd called them to the table and a lull had settled
over the initial attempt at conversation, Susie couldn't help
bringing up Goodwin again.

"Don't you think we ought to be worried, Mr. Swift? I
mean, what if Mr. Goodwin were to start bothering us?"

"Us?" I said, meaning to point out that Susie was talking as though Goodwin had fallen in love with her. She
ignored me. Dad mixed his pasta with his fork, trying to get
it to the proper consistency. He'd never liked spaghetti
much, and would have complained in the old days if Mom
had made it for him.

"Why would he do that?"

"Because he's nuts," Susie said. "And you know what?
Joan looks a bit like Stephanie Rush? Have you ever
noticed that?"

"What?" I tried to act appalled, but was actually a little
flattered. The two of them sat there studying my face.

"Nooooo," Dad finally said.

"She does. Her mouth, I think. A little bit."

Dad awkwardly rolled his fork, imitating Susie, trying
to wind on a mouthful of noodles.

"Didn't seem nuts to me. Sure knew his way around a tractor. Have you been over to visit your mother lately?"

"No. I'm busy."

"Yeah, well, she's your mother."

Susie looked at her plate. She was on Dad's side when it came to this recurring discussion. I could not make them understand how much energy Mom took (though Dad, of all people, should have known). It wasn't that I didn't want to see her; I just didn't have the strength.

"So you invited Goodwin over to fix your machinery?"

"Did your mother ever get her radiator fixed?"

"I don't know. Should she call Goodwin?"

I got a stern-father look for that comment.

"He helped me," Dad said.

"He never came around when I was old enough to remember."

"Nope," Dad said. "Stopped comin'."

"'Cause Mom ordered him never to set foot on the place again?"

I watched him guide a forkful to his mouth, then suck in the loose ends and wipe the sauce from his lips with the side of his hand.

"Mighta been. That would show good sense on his part, wouldn't it?"

Susie giggled, then blushed.

"Oh, yeah, he's a sensible person," I said.

Dad granted his own wit a huge grin.

"You know what's really weird?" Susie reached over and pinched my arm. "*She* never even recognized him."

Dad shrugged.

"He looks about like the next guy, I guess."

And Dad was right. The living Goodwin is altogether different from the fellow in the newspapers. That guy was a famous nut. This guy was just some farmer. There was the nasty squint of his eyes, but that was normal for farmers: they're generally all a bit paranoid. Why wouldn't they be? When it came right down to it, Goodwin wasn't much different from Dad. He certainly didn't seem very crazy. There were plenty of library regulars who were much stranger than him.

For instance, there was the man who always came in, winter or summer, with his shirt wide open and one hand in his pants. He'd sit at a table in the back and stare at Wanda as she squirmed nervously in her chair behind the information desk. He was in love with Wanda. He'd always ask her what information she had for him today. I was glad he left me alone. I'd only ever spoken to him once, when he stopped at the front desk at closing time, after Wanda'd had to tell him it was time to leave; he asked me if I liked Sundays—it was Sunday. It's a difficult thing to converse with a man with one hand in his pants, so I simply told him yes, and he assured me that he liked Sundays too, and then he left (only pausing briefly to check his reflection in the glass of the book display) apparently satisfied that he had succeeded in proving to me what a great deal we had in common.

And then there was the woman who came in two or three times every day, but in all the years I worked there I never heard her say one word. She walked like a zombie, her head so rigid you'd think her neck was welded to her shoulders, only sometimes you'd catch her looking at you out of the corner of her eye with a stare that made you feel she was sizing you up for a coffin, and as soon as you'd catch her eye she'd look away. She'd find a book and sit at a table scanning the pictures with her jack-fish stare—they were always picture books. When she was finished she'd leave the book on the table and walk out. She never checked out a book. She never spoke. She never smiled.

And then there was Hector. When he came for his daily visit I'd always ask him how he was and he'd always say, "I don't know. I'm not a doctor." And he'd smile. He'd order a book on Gaelic, and the diaries of a sixteenth-century French peasant, and the Warren Commission report, and *The Thousand and One Nights* of Scheherazade, and a Taoist guide to oral sex, and all the time he'd have this queer little smirk on his face, like he'd just murdered your mother but you didn't know about it yet. He'd ask you if you needed an opium pipe for the book display on China. And he'd smile. He'd ask you if you knew a good psychiatrist in town. And he'd smile. He'd ask you if you knew what happened to the wine that the British troops confiscated from the Iraqi soldiers during the Gulf War. And he'd smile. And then he'd leave. And a half-hour later he'd phone back and order two more books: de Maupassant's *Collected Stories* and a biography of Hitler.

"They learned a lot from Hitler, didn't they," Hector'd say, and when you asked him, "Who?" he'd pause for a moment, as though surprised, before he'd reply, "Everybody."

Anyway, my point is that there's a lot stranger people than Darwin Andrew Goodwin, even in Broken Head.

That weekend I made the mistake of letting Susie get to the phone first and, wouldn't you know it, it was Mom, wondering if I'd been kidnapped or brutally murdered or joined the local chapter of Friends of Satan or why else hadn't I called her or returned her messages? Susie told her she guessed I'd been busy and maybe a bit preoccupied with the fact that Darwin Andrew Goodwin had fallen in love with me. Then she called me to the phone.

"You phone the police immediately!"

"Why? He never came back. He hasn't bothered me."

"Oh, fine then. Just wait until he does. Just wait until they're hauling you away in a body bag. Just wait until ..."

"Okay, okay, I'll call them."

"You do that!"

"All right. I will."

"Who knows what the man's capable of."

"I said I would."

"This is horrible. Imagine what he might do to you. And all because your father insisted on running that stupid farm, two miles up the road from the greatest psychopath in the entire known universe...."

"Mom! Don't bring the farm into this."

"You call them, now!"

"All right. I will."

I hung up on her and left the phone off the hook.

Susie kept bothering me to call the police, so finally I told her I had and that they'd said to let them know if I had the least intimation that he might be watching our house. For months after, Susie would periodically slip to the window and lift a corner of the curtain, peering out at our deserted street for any sign of suspicious life.

That all happened before Jason walked into the library one day in April. I should have called the police about *him*.

At any rate, there we were in Laurie Johnson's parents' bed, and Jason was watching the news. Fortunately, it wasn't to be an ongoing ritual, though there was one other time when he found a copy of the *Guardian Weekly* on somebody's dresser and started reading about the European perspective on last week's developments in the fish wars. When I complained he told me it was kind of a compliment: like enjoying fine brandy after a gourmet meal.

On that first day I realized that he realized just what a pitifully inexperienced small-town girl I actually was, and I got up to scuttle away and only stopped a moment to say, "Doesn't any news ever happen here?"

And Jason said, "Goodwin. Nothing except Goodwin."

It took me a moment to register what and whom he meant.

"Darwin Andrew Goodwin?"

Jason didn't even grunt, his whole being funnelled through his eyes and sucked into that television tube.

"Darwin Andrew Goodwin?" I repeated. "You've heard of him?"

"Of course I've heard of him."

"Have you done any stories about him?"

"No. He hasn't been arrested since I moved here. I tried to interview him for an article for *Saturday Night*, but he wouldn't talk to me. Got all indignant and nasty. Rednecked ..."

A commercial came on and he flicked over to see the baseball score. I was about to go search out my clothes.

"Isn't that funny? I know Darwin Goodwin. In fact, Susie says he's in love with me."

Jason turned and met my eyes, his mouth open in a perfect circle.

"Pardon me?"

"He was our neighbour."

"Your neighbour? He's a farmer."

"He lived just up the road. A couple miles."

"Oh. A couple miles? And … and Susie said … what?"

"Well, when he came into the library once, he said he used to think I was the prettiest little girl in the world."

"The prettiest … in the world? Really? Why? When?"

"I don't know. A year ago."

"Is that really what your friend said? In love with you?"

"Yeah. Love."

"Really? So, he might talk to you? You could interview him?"

"Well … I don't do interviews. I'm a librarian."

"No, but … you could talk to him. For me. Do you know what *Saturday Night* pays? I'd give you a cut."

"Really? *Saturday Night*. Well … I guess? If you want? Do you think … what if he gets the wrong idea?"

"What idea?"

"I don't know. The idea that I like him. The idea that I love him. It's not as though he hasn't done it before."

Jason considered this carefully.

"Yeah, you're right," he finally said. "It might be dangerous." And now he looked like I'd told him he would not live until morning.

"I could do it," I said. "I'm not scared of him."

"No. You're right. It's a bad idea."

"No, really. I don't mind."

"Forget it. He's old news, anyway. *Saturday Night* probably wouldn't even be interested any more. Unless he gets himself arrested again … or something."

He reached up to brush a lock of my hair behind my ear. I thought maybe he was about to ask me something else about Goodwin, but instead he said, "How many loved your moments of glad grace, and loved your beauty, with love both false and true, but one man loved the pilgrim soul in you, and loved the changing sorrows of your face."

And then he kissed me. And then he kissed me again. He forgot all about the news of the world and the baseball game.

Over the course of that spring and summer I must have met Jason a dozen times, sneaking up strange driveways in darkness, or slouching below dashboard level so no one could see he had a passenger.

Susie was immediately suspicious.

"Where are you off to?"

"Just for a walk. Maybe I'll go over and see Mom."

She flicked over the page of her *Vogue*, then hit me with those mannequin eyes she was imitating from the supermodels.

"Really?"

"Yeah. Maybe. Maybe I'll just walk. I need to stretch my legs."

"I'll come along."

She jumped to her feet to show that she was ready to follow me, already knowing what I'd say.

"I don't think so. Listen, sorry, but I just need a bit of space."

She stung me again with her eyes, and then slowly, dramatically, lowered herself to our orange floral couch. My orange floral bed.

"Yeah," she said, licking her finger and flicking over another page of her magazine. "Don't stretch your legs *too* far."

There was this one time, a Friday night, Susie and I were at the cowboy bar in the Elite Hotel —the cowboys all pronounced it "E-Light"—sipping shooters between vodka-and-Sevens, when Jason and his artsy friend with the spiky hair walked through the off-sale door. (If you're from a city, it may surprise you that Jason had been able to find an artsy friend in Broken Head, but the fact is there's probably every kind of person in Broken Head that there is in any city, except there's only one or two of him or her, so that instead of belonging to some artificial community, she or he has no choice but to participate in a real one.)

I caught Jason's eye accidentally before I could look the other way, and the next thing I knew, to my considerable shock, as he didn't like to acknowledge me in public, he was standing at the table, introducing his friend to me.

"Barry, this is ummmm ... Joan, right?"

Barry extended his hand to me and I took it. "Yeah, you're the librarian, right? Best front page the *Standard* ever had."

"Thanks," I said, and introduced Susie, who pasted on a pout before managing to nod. Barry still hadn't returned my hand.

"Well, we should get goin'," Jason said.

"No, no, let's stop for one or two here," Barry was already lowering himself into a chair.

"I don't think—" Jason started to say.

"Awww, come on. What's the rush? Carol's not missin' you. These married guys," he rolled his eyes at me.

Seeing that Barry had already ensconced himself, Jason reluctantly sat down and tried his best to look bored while Barry flirted unmercifully with me. I must admit that I didn't discourage him, though I wasn't the least bit interested in someone who was even more affected than Jason but didn't carry it off nearly so well, possibly owing to the fact that he'd never been farther afield than one term at the University of Regina. Christmas dropout.

"You remind me of someone. Who is it you look like?"

"The Virgin Mary?" I offered.

"I'm not even Catholic," he snorted, then turned, for the first time, to Susie. "Who does she look like?"

"Herself. She looks exactly like Joan Swift and nothing like anyone else, 'cause she's one hundred per cent real, every part of her."

Susie was looking at Jason, not Barry, when she said this.

"Well, I guess that puts me in my place," Barry said, pushing his Buddy Holly frames up to the bridge of his nose (Jason later told me that the glasses were not prescription, but were meant to give Barry a more intellectual look: they had raised his marks by twenty points in grade twelve, but failed to do their magic in university). "But you're right. You're absolutely right. She's one hundred per cent herself. Every part of her."

As a toast to this platitude, he took a pull from his beer.

"Can we change the subject? I feel like I'm being dismembered."

Susie slid forward in her chair and actually pinched Barry's arm.

"Why don't you ask her out?"

He was still in the process of swallowing that pull on

his beer, and being pinched by Susie made it go the wrong way, sending him into a helpless coughing fit. When he finally managed to get control of himself, face red from embarrassment and lack of oxygen, he could only squeak, "We *are* out."

I kicked Susie in the ankle. She gritted her teeth and kept talking.

"No, I mean it. You two'd make a great couple. You'd be perfect together." Again, she said this to Jason, who was no longer looking bored.

"What *are* you?" Jason asked. "Her *pimp*?"

Susie replied by attempting to throw her vodka-and-Seven in his face, but her aim was off and she hit Barry.

During the ensuing scene—which involved a drunken old cowboy, who happened to be ambling by on the way to the john, grabbing Barry by his spiky hair and pulling back his neck so far I thought his head might snap right off before I was able, with Susie's help, to convince him to let the poor boy go—Jason calmly rose and walked out of the bar. Very likely the old cowboy would not even remember Jason had ever been there.

Afterwards, the cowboy wouldn't leave us alone—he'd fallen deeply in love with Susie when he saw her hurl her drink—and so we had to leave.

As we walked the four blocks toward the sports bar Susie was pouting and wouldn't speak to me and so I said, "That was so weird. You don't like that Jason guy, do you?"

"Do you?" she asked. "He called you a whore."

"Not really. Well, maybe he was jealous."

She leapt at the bait.

"Why would he be jealous?"

"I don't know. Maybe he and Barry are a couple."

Susie stopped, right there in front of the empty Beaver Lumber parking lot.

"You think so?"

I shrugged.

"Maybe."

She started walking again.

"No," she said.

"Well, there is such as thing as gay people, you know? Even in Broken Head."

"I *know*." She was insulted. "Like Reverend Porter, for instance."

I missed a step, but managed to get back into pace before Susie noticed.

"Reverend Porter's gay?"

"Isn't she?" Susie asked.

"I don't know. Is she?"

"I don't know. I just assumed."

We kept walking, silent, while I considered the evidence and realized that Susie was probably right. Reverend Porter, minister of the United Church, a woman of the cloth, led a double life. And if Susie had reached such an assumption, then likely many people knew; nevertheless, Reverend Porter was accepted by her congregation. A wonder of toleration, right here in small-town redneck West. Not much was said, and it had to go on just below the surface so as not to raise the ire of the vocal minority who would make a problem of such things, but it was there just the same. People coping with their needs, their differences, their crippled relationships. It had been going on for centuries. At that moment, it struck me as a kind of permission for my own duplicity. I wanted to thank Susie. I wanted to dump my whole other self on the sidewalk at her feet.

"If he was in love with him he wouldn't have deserted him that way, would he? What kind of guy deserts a friend that way?"

"Are you kidding? If he'd jumped on that cowboy, what would all the other cowboys have done? Somebody'd likely be burying him."

Susie pouted some more.

"He's such a snob," Susie finally said. "He thinks he's better than everybody. You can tell. He's no better than anybody else. I don't trust him."

I shrugged. "What's to trust?"

Unfortunately, when it came to the Warhol, Jason was not satisfied with allowing the unconventional to go on under the surface. That's why, if you ask me, it was Jason, and not Goodwin, who was responsible for its destruction. He'd taken it upon himself "to raise the profile of the arts in the community" by doing a story on each new show at the gallery. Darwin Andrew Goodwin, like so many others in Broken Head, had never visited the gallery in his life. He walked right by it that day he came into the library to photocopy his legal documents—the gallery is in the same building as the library—but never in his entire life had he ever gone inside to look at the pictures hanging on the walls, and he never would have known about Mr. Warhol's silkscreen if Jason hadn't written about it in the *Standard*. He intentionally singled out the print of the topless Stephanie Rush for mention because he "thought it might provoke some interest in the arts."

It did. There were two letters to the editor claiming that such a picture might lead to child abuse or worse. And then there was Goodwin's call.

"Warwick? This is Goodwin. Darwin Goodwin. Meet me at the art gallery in half an hour and I'll show you what I think of your work of art."

In his book Jason claims that he was surprised by the call. It is true that Goodwin had refused to talk to Jason many times before, had even tried to get an injunction to prevent Jason from contacting him in any way—the same sort of injunction that Stephanie Rush had used against Goodwin— but the courts wouldn't award him one, leaving him no recourse except his muttered threats of what he would do if Jason bothered him again.

But I still don't believe that Jason was surprised by Goodwin's call. If he were honest he would admit that he had been calculating Darwin Andrew Goodwin's reaction when he wrote that article. I wouldn't even be surprised if Jason called him and told him to read it.

It was definitely the most exciting thing ever to happen at the library. When I left for lunch that day I noticed Jason's car parked across the street, him sitting behind the wheel. I walked over and he rolled down the window. His camera was in his lap.

"What are you up to?"

"Working on a story."

I surveyed the street. On a power line a couple of magpies perched, watching some children playing road hockey in a driveway. The wind scattered yellow leaves across lawns and deposited them along the curbs where they might eventually wash away and clog the storm drains at the corners. If we got another big rain like we'd had in July the water might inch up toward the library door before the city crew could get there to lift the iron traps. But the sky was clear. The hum of a million combines gulping up wheat was in the air. An elderly man was walking his dog, a golden retriever, and when Fido spotted the two boys swiping at the ball with their sticks he started to bark and the magpies took flight.

"I'd lead off with the dog," I said. "That'll grab their attention."

"Pardon?"

"For your story. I'd lead off with the dog. Come to think of it, his owner might even be carrying a scoop."

Jason smiled. "Bye-bye."

He rolled up the window. I stood there for a moment, staring at him through that grimy glass until, with that same smile and a couple of patronizing flicks of his hand, he motioned me away. I didn't think much of it. He never liked to be seen with me in public.

By the time I got back from lunch there were two police cars parked in front of the library. Jason was sitting in the back seat of one of them, calmly talking, while a cop took notes. His face was covered with what looked like blood. I wanted to open the door and get in with him, but I knew that wouldn't be a good idea. Instead I went into the library. I remember thinking that if I didn't I'd be late. I was expecting more blood.

Ivan was standing at the door to the gallery talking to another cop. "Why in hell didn't that stupid moron of a reporter do something? He stands there taking pictures. Why the hell didn't he do something to try and stop him?

This is art. A precious work of art. He stands there taking photographs while someone destroys an irreplaceable object."

Darwin Andrew Goodwin had used a can of red spray paint that he'd bought to touch up one of his tractors: Massey-Ferguson red. Jason followed him into the library and snapped three photographs of him spray-painting over Stephanie Rush's breasts. When Goodwin was finished with the Warhol, he turned the spray can on Jason.

Those photographs made Jason more money than he'd earn in a year at the *Standard*. He even managed to sell the last shot, in which the frame was filled completely with a warm red glow.

*S*tephanie Rush, the object of Goodwin's dreams, remains the unparalleled pride of Venus, Alberta. Their town council long ago erected a billboard on the outskirts, across the road from the livestock yards, announcing to all pilgrims that they have indeed attained the site of her birth, and the local drugstore sells drinking glasses with the name of the town emblazoned across her leering image beside the My Parents Went to Venus and All they Brought Me Was This Shirt *T-shirts.*

Venus is one of a billion Prairie villages facing imminent extinction. It exists, barely, just north of a great hole in the map that is a Canadian Forces base still occupied by British troops. To get there you have to dare to leave the Trans-Canada about an hour west of Broken Head, and wind your way around the potholes along various tertiary highways for another two hours northwest, until you might actually begin to believe you've crossed most of the ninety-three million miles to the sun. Finally, slowly, out of the horizon, the great white teeth of

Stephanie Rush begin to rise into the sky. After all these centuries, the goddess of love still lives. The vision can only be described as sublime.

A green sign says Venus 1.

Most Americans don't realize that Stephanie Rush was Canadian. She lived in Los Angeles for the last thirty years of her life. Canadians, however, retain a claim on all of our movie stars, no matter how long ago they left Canada. Perhaps we do so because part of the appeal of fame is how it brushes against our small lives, granting us significance, almost in the same way a lover affirms us by conceding, in need for us, that we are worthy of love. We must look south to find this connection. To remain in Canada is to resign yourself to a pale imitation of fame. If you are on this side of the border, you must be satisfied with the fifteen minutes Mr. Warhol promised you.

More than for her acting talents, Stephanie Rush was famous for her breasts. Her husband, the celebrated Hollywood director Russel Burlitz, liked to call her a physical genius. Stephanie herself, ever the modest Prairie girl, insisted that her only stroke of genius was marrying the great director. It is strange that with fifty million men in love with Stephanie Rush, Darwin Goodwin's little passion would make him famous. But Darwin Goodwin could not keep the songs of his heart silent; he displayed his devotion in ways that made people everywhere tell his story. He has been persecuted for his

love: arrested at least a dozen times. And why? An old story.
Darwin Goodwin's love was unrequited. An old story, but one
with consequences so tragic that the ancient poets might have
invented it themselves.

An excerpt from
Make Believe Love
By Jason Warwick

[Monday, June 12th]

Worked late again last night and the phone woke me this morning. Mom. She refuses to visit, has all but disowned me, but still calls every now and then to remind me how I have ruined her life along with my own.

"You have no idea what people are saying, do you?"

"They're not saying much of anything any more, Mom. They've moved on to the next catastrophe."

"I'm not talking about the television. I'm talking about people here. My friends. The people I have to live with."

"What are they saying, Mom?"

"Well, I don't know exactly, because they don't say it to me, of course. But I can well imagine."

"So you don't really know if they're saying anything at all."

"Oh, they are. And, of course, they blame me. They always blame the mother. I just don't understand what I did wrong. How could you and your father do anything to associate our name with that man's?"

"You could always change your name and move somewhere else."

"I just might have to."

In the end she agreed to come to dinner on Thursday, so Dad and I can show her how well we're getting along.

I bit my tongue so many times in that conversation. I am trying to find a place for her even if she no longer has one for me, because I know I really have hurt her. And as Dad keeps telling me, she *is* my mother.

But I thought mothers were supposed to forgive you no matter what you did. Don't mothers even forgive their serial killer sons? So why can't my mother forgive me?

I realize that with all the awful stories out there, I can never make her understand unless she knows the real story of Goodwin. I have been reluctant to tell anything of his past. It's ground that's been covered so often before, and always with such sickeningly exploitative treatments. But each time I consider avoiding it, I run smack dab against all the lies that Jason's and other books have already spread. And so I find myself left with no choice but to give you my own version.

At any rate, it shouldn't take long, which suits me. It's hot. Outside, I mean. I can't take another sixteen-hour day. I'll just dash this off and maybe go for a swim in the creek.

Darwin Andrew Goodwin was born at the Broken Head Union Hospital on a blustery day in February of 1953. There had been warnings that some weather was coming and his father had trucked his mother off to town before it hit, figuring that a blizzard would likely be the time little Darwin would choose to squirm into the world. And he was right....

But that's too far back. No one's interested in the details of Darwin's childhood and youth.

That's not true, either. The problem is that I can't possibly give any details without them being psychoanalyzed for how he was moulded into the monster he becomes. The truth is that he was a kid who grew up on a farm, a bit lonely, a bit isolated. He would have made up games that he could play by himself in order to keep amused. This lack of external stimulation often results in an overactive and deviant imagination. Like mine. Like all of us farm kids.

I'll tell you what: if we're gonna talk dirt, then let's dig in. Bear with me. It's but the stuff that TV movies are made of. I'm feeling a bit tainted already, even just thinking about how to get started. But if Jason can do it, I'm sure that I can do better.

It all began when Darwin Goodwin went to see a movie at the Lyric Theatre way back in the early seventies, before the Lyric closed and reopened as a disco. Imagine him sitting there in the dark, cramming his popcorn into his mouth and washing it down with his Coca-Cola, while up on the screen Stephanie Rush thrusts those breasts at him, those Technicolor breasts that span twenty feet of the Lyric's screen; and then, during a love scene, that funny little director husband of hers makes the foolish mistake of having Stephanie speak those three little words that have destroyed more lives than all the cocaine in the world— had her say "I love you" directly into the camera, to make it seem like Stephanie was telling each one of those fifty million men out there that she loved him, really him, and not Burt Reynolds, the big guy with the fake hair who was playing the part of the man she was really supposed to be pretending to say those words to. It's easy enough to figure why the funny little director chose to shoot the scene that way: because it was less painful to have his wife profess her love to fifty million faceless men than to have her say it to Burt Reynolds. The funny little director, you see, according to Stephanie's parents, had always been rabidly jealous. But the plan backfired on him, because young Darwin Goodwin, sitting in the dark with his popcorn and his Coke, could not help believing what those huge lips were telling him. She loved him. She couldn't possibly live without him. And why shouldn't she love him? She wasn't like those other movie stars: she was a real flesh-and-blood woman who was brought up on a farm near Venus. What could be more natural than for a farm girl from Alberta to fall in love with a farmer from Saskatchewan?

Darwin Goodwin's little fantasy wouldn't have caused anyone too much trouble if he'd been satisfied with keeping it between himself and a glossy photo in a magazine. But no. That night when he got home from the Lyric, he decided to phone Stephanie herself and let her know how he felt about her. After all, it wasn't that late in Los Angeles: they're an hour behind Saskatchewan. Unfortunately, the directory assistance people wanted to know what part of Los Angeles she lived in, and when Darwin dug that up in one of his magazines and called back, it turned out there were no less than fourteen S. Rushes in Malibu alone. He gave her husband's name, but there were none of him.

Darwin Goodwin didn't give up easily though, and the very next day he set off on a crusade to the very patch of ground where Stephanie was raised. He had no problem finding the farm. The clerk at the grocery store in Venus was only too glad to give him directions, pleased that she could claim a piece of Stephanie Rush's early years: Stephanie was her best friend in grade three, and Stephanie had predicted way back then that she would be a movie star one day. How could Stephanie Rush have known, when she was only eight years old? But she did. Even without the breasts she knew she was destined for greatness. But, no, no, you're wrong, Stephanie was not one for dolls. Magazines, yes, but not dolls. She threw the clerk's Barbie into a campfire once, and then complained about the smell she made when she burned. They were not friends after that, though the clerk forgives her now, certainly. There is nothing if there is not forgiveness.

When Darwin arrived at the farm, Mr. Rush was in his shop fussing over his front-end loader: he was constantly pouring oil through the thing because the gasket on the oil pan had been leaking for years, but you couldn't take off the oil pan to replace the gasket without removing the front axle and Mr. Rush—"Ernie! Call me Ernie!"—never had the time or the hands he needed to do the job: he and Mrs. Rush had only been blessed with the one daughter, Stephanie, and the man she had married was not the son a farmer could find useful.

Coincidentally, Darwin had exactly the same front-end loader and had had exactly the same problem with the gasket on the oil pan, so, after commiserating on the decline of American engineering, Darwin led Ernie through the steps in dismantling and reassembling the machine: you could use the hydraulics on the bucket to hold up the front end while you took off the axle, so long as you had a few blocks in place for safety's sake. They were finished by suppertime:

Darwin cut the gasket out of a roll of cork himself, over Ernie's protestations that he could save him the trouble by running to town for a store-bought one. Ernie never cut them himself any more, didn't even remember how many years ago he'd bought the cork. The piece of paper inside the roll said the cork had come all the way from Portugal, which is where that queer little director had taken Stephanie for the summer. Far be it that they could come to Alberta. The little nose-wipe would have none of that. He was scared to death of animals and big machines. He was scared to death of real-life people, like Ernie and Margaret, Stephanie's own flesh and blood, and the only way they could see their beloved daughter was by taking their lives in their hands and going down to that insane city and staying in that little turd's mansion, which was about as comfortable as living in a museum, added to which you had to put up with the little prick's constant slights. He seemed to think they were so stupid they couldn't see what he thought of them— couldn't understand his snide demeaning comments. In spite of his behaviour they were always polite and friendly with him, of course. They knew their manners.

Margaret Rush confirmed all of this over the supper table, only using somewhat less colourful language to describe the funny little director. It was just too bad that Stephanie'd never found a decent man like Darwin to marry: a man who spoke plainly and knew his way around a tractor. Certainly they'd be glad to give him Stephanie's address and telephone number, though they couldn't promise her husband would make him welcome there when he happened to be passing through Los Angeles, as Darwin said he would be this winter.

"Going down for a few days at Disneyland."

They all had to agree that there was no more worth-while place in the world than Disneyland.

After supper they made him stay and admire Ernie's model railway, which took up most of the basement. For a while he wondered if they might even ask him to spend the night there, in the very house where Stephanie grew up, perhaps even in the very bed she'd slept in, but they never asked, simply because it never occurred to them that he might have accepted if they had, and he couldn't suggest it. He knew his manners.

He drove all night and was home the next morning. His mother was furious that he'd risked his life by driving all night, was furious that he'd gone away in the first place without telling her where he was going, but he told her he guessed he couldn't always be pleasing his mother any more, that he'd gone to meet the parents of the girl he was going to marry, so maybe she'd better get used to the idea of another woman being around, and that meant a lot of getting used to, because he wasn't going to be one to let his mother tell his wife what to do. She wanted to know how come she hadn't met this woman if her parents were already meeting him: was he ashamed of his old mother? He only grunted at that and wouldn't say anything more. The breakfast she made for them was consumed in obstinate silence and then he went out to get started on the summer fallowing, with her yelling after him that he'd better get a couple of hours' rest at least or he'd fall asleep on the tractor and wouldn't wake up until he'd cultivated clear to the border.

He wrote a couple of letters addressed to the villa in Portugal where Stephanie and her husband were staying, but they were answered by her fan club in Los Angeles, offering him a membership for fifteen American dollars, which included a laminated membership card, a list of facts about her life and career, and a signed photograph that he hung in the kitchen though his mother protested that she wouldn't have pornographic pictures staring at her while she cooked. By now it was clear that this was the woman he'd spoken about that morning: the girl he meant to marry. At first she dismissed the whole thing as another one of his delusions, just like all the girls from school he'd told her he was going to marry. There had even been a few he'd asked out, but she'd put a stop to it before it was too late. She knew enough about young men in love to know nothing would get done around here if he started romancing. It would have been all right if his father were alive, but there was only him to do the work and, consequently, there was no time for girls.

So at first she was only slightly annoyed by the silly infatuation, but when a letter arrived from the girl's parents, and she finally uncovered it in a new hiding place behind the wall lamp in his bedroom, and read that "we are so glad to hear that Stephanie has responded to you so enthusiastically," and that "you seemed to us like the son we never had, and we sincerely think it would be a blessing if Stephanie would give up the false life she has for a simple and loving man such as yourself," his mother began to worry.

When he came in from the field she confronted him with the letter.

"This is a married woman. *This* is a married woman," she told him over and over again, stabbing her finger at Stephanie Rush, who bared an indecent amount of her ample cleavage at them from between the refrigerator and the wooden plaque that said This Is the Tomorrow We Worried about Yesterday and All Is Well.

"Not happily married," Darwin told her.

"I can't believe what I'm hearing," his mother said. "I can't believe what you're suggesting. If your father heard you say something like that he'd lock you in your room for a year."

"But Dad's not here, and this is the seventies," Darwin shot back at her.

"Oh! Don't tell me that my own son has turned into one of those hippies! With no more morals than an animal!"

She was sitting behind her sewing machine, patching a pair of his workpants, the letter spread open on the table. Next to the letter was a rack of chocolate-chip cookies, still hot from the oven. Darwin picked up the letter and, with a cold calculatedness she had never seen in him before, paused a moment to select a cookie, then marched out of the room.

She was losing him. She'd lost his father so many years ago she had trouble imagining him any more, even believing he had once existed. He'd drowned in his own granary: dropped in through the cap to check his flax (flax was an experiment she'd warned him against) for beetles and was sucked under like a miser drowning in his own gold. The boy was only sixteen when his father died. She wasn't about to let *him* go under without a fight.

He phoned Stephanie Rush's house a dozen times, but it was never she who answered and it didn't matter if he left a message that he was a friend of her parents, the calls were never returned. Ernie and Margaret weren't surprised by this when he told them: Stephanie's husband wouldn't want her having anything to do with friends of her parents. The more he thought it over, the clearer it became. There was only one solution: he'd have to go to Los Angeles and see her.

There is no reason to believe that Darwin Goodwin felt any different, as he pulled his Fargo pick-up truck out of the driveway and onto the highway that headed south from Broken Head, than Stephanie Rush had one day years before when she had left behind the little Alberta town named after Earth's sister planet. He was on his way to the city where angels held up lamp-posts on every corner—the end of the rainbow, the promised land, the dream machine, the capital of West, photographed so often it had dissolved into a state of mind, its tangibility just out of frame, where shutters and synapses never quite close. He may have considered how the history of that city was not so different from the history of Broken Head or Venus or any of the other millions of towns that dotted the West: every one of them was built by people running away from something, running toward their dreams. He may have reflected that the original boosters of all those towns had the same aspirations as the original boosters of Los Angeles, but that LA was the shining success that rose up like a beacon in the centre of all of their tiny failures. It is even possible that Darwin Goodwin wondered, as the highway reeled away behind him, if he would ever return to Broken Head, or if he too would become a dream that the lonely citizens of the little Prairie town would watch on winter evenings in the blue flicker of their living rooms.

What he found at the other end of the highway was disappointment. As he neared the great city the freeway became a free-for-all where he was the butt of every aggression—one glance at the indecipherable word on the licence plate and they all wanted to squash the hunk of metal that had had the audacity to crawl all the way from the jungles of South America and clog up a lane and a half of the long road between the office and home. It made him bitter when he considered that in Broken Head he had once witnessed the mere sight of a blue licence plate drawing a crowd of well-wishers, all calling, "How ya doin', California?"

It was the dirtiest place in the world: dirty streets, dirty people, dirty air. The gaudy neon signs looked embarrassed in the smog-yellow light of day. He was crossing a street in Hollywood, searching forlornly for traces of celebrity, when he saw a black man lying on the stone steps of the crumbling ruins of what must once have been a library. There was something unmistakable in his stillness, something Darwin had only witnessed once before in a human being—when he'd dug his father from the flax in that bin, had touched his shoulder to wake him—but had never forgotten. Darwin knelt and touched the man's cold skin. People just kept walking past as though they didn't notice either of them. As far as they were concerned, Darwin was as dead as the other man. Only one raggedy woman teetering against a wall sensed something was wrong and came and touched the cold skin too, then ran away in panic. Darwin rose and walked back to his truck.

Luckily, there was a bus tour advertising a glimpse of the estate that Stephanie Rush shared with the funny little director. "Glimpse" was an overstatement, but Darwin marked the street on his map and, when the tour was over, drove straight to the X.

There were stone walls, ten feet high, surrounding the entire property. They had a couple of acres. The steel gates at the front entrance were equipped with an intercom system and when he buzzed it a man answered. The funny little director? No, the voice was much too officious. Some kind of servant.

"State your name."

"I'm here to see Miss Rush."

"State your name, please."

"Darwin. I'm here to see Miss Rush."

"State your full name."

"Darwin Andrew Goodwin. I'm a friend of Miss Rush's parents."

"Our records show no appointment for any Goodwin."

"No. I don't have any appointment. Just dropping by."

"I'm sorry, sir. You'll have to make an appointment with Ms. Rush in order to be admitted to the grounds."

"But I'm a friend of her Mom and Dad's."

"I'm sorry, sir."

"Well, I'd like to make an appointment then."

"That'll be fine."

"How about tomorrow?"

"Pardon me, sir?"

"Can I make an appointment for tomorrow?"

"We don't arrange appointments, sir. We're security. You'll have to arrange an appointment through Ms. Rush's agency."

"Her what?"

"Her agency."

"Well, could you give me the name of her agency?"

And so they did. And so Darwin tried to make an appointment through the agency. They told him they'd let him know. He left them the number of his motel room, then sat for forty-eight hours straight, watching the television—there were so many channels it would have taken half a dozen people a week to witness one day's programming—afraid even to go to sleep for fear that he might not wake when the phone rang. At last, he called back.

"I'm sorry, Ms. Rush has never heard of you."

"I'm a friend of her parents. Her parents must have told her about me."

"No, I'm sorry, Ms. Rush has never heard of you."

"Well, tell her to call her parents."

"I'm sorry, sir, but Ms. Rush doesn't know you. Ms. Rush is a very busy woman. Ms. Rush has no interest in meeting with you."

He tried phoning Stephanie's parents, hoping they could somehow help, but he hadn't even got through explaining the situation when Margaret interrupted him: "I don't think it's a good idea that you phone here any more." He asked to speak to Ernie. "Ernie doesn't want to speak to you. Please don't call here any more."

She hung up in his ear.

He went to a bar and got drunk on watery American beer. He wandered up and down streets, raining curses on the ugly city. And it might have ended there. He might have gone back to his motel, thrown his suitcase in his truck and gone home.

But he didn't. Darwin Goodwin was not the kind of man to resign his love so easily.

A s fate would have it, I met Joan Swift early on in my stay in Broken Head. Despite the protestations of my editor at The Broken Head Standard I took it upon myself to use my position to raise the profile of the few cultural institutions that Broken Head did have to offer: the community college, the little theatre, various musical organizations (mostly choirs associated with one church or another), the museum, the art gallery and, of course, the library.

The Broken Head Public Library had for years been starved for cash by a philistine town council. They offered a dismally small stock of books and magazines, and an inexperienced staff who struggled to run the operation with archaic equipment. "Clay tablet and chisel," as Joan Swift herself put it when I interviewed her for an article about the facility.

The mayor, Mr. Ernest Howarth, had appointed himself to the library board because he was disgusted by the fact that he had to pay money on his property taxes for a library he never *used. Spending ratepayers' dollars so that other people could read books sounded suspiciously like Communism to His Worship. He had come up with a plan to raise funds by selling the public library to a private developer who would turn it into an "Elderly Care Facility." (Caring for the aged was one of the major industries in Broken Head.) The profits from the sale could then be used for more worthwhile pursuits—like constructing a badly needed new hockey rink.*

The mayor hoped to avoid any unnecessary attention to his plan until the sale was finalized. They held a secret board meeting, not inviting the media, but a single conscientious board member leaked the information to me. I was afraid that the editor, a friend of the mayor's, would kill the story, so I included it in a "City Happenings" column that I knew the editor always neglected to read, due to his onerous workload: he often tried to help out the sales staff by spending his afternoons selling ad space to one or another brewery representative who frequented the Corral Room at the Elite Hotel.

The response to my story was heated enough to scuttle the mayor's plans and from then on he and my editor regarded me as an enemy. I later discovered that the story had the even more unfortunate repercussion of making me a hero in Joan Swift's eyes.

Joan Swift had only just graduated from high school when she landed a job as a library clerk. She claimed to have won the job because she "loved books," which certainly made her more qualified than any of her competition. She grew up on a farm

just two miles down the road from Darwin Andrew Goodwin,
and apparently he had been something of a favourite "Uncle" of
hers. Her father, a farmer who had only recently lost his land
to the banks, recalled Goodwin "bouncing Joan on his knee
when he came to help fix the machinery."

Considering the proximity of their farms, it seems likely
that Joan Swift and Goodwin carried on some kind of intimacy
over the course of her adolescence, though this cannot be veri-
fied, as Swift, like her mentor Darwin Goodwin, has refused to
talk to any reporters, and her family will only defensively insist
that as a teenager "she had nothing to do with that man."

On first sight, Joan Swift somewhat resembled the stereo-
typically demure librarian, but her fiery shock of alarmingly red
hair hinted at her sharp tongue, and the depth of her blue eyes
should have warned me of an inner life that was—to put it
mildly—rather complex. None of that was revealed to me until
later, though. On our first meeting, when I interviewed her for the
aforementioned newspaper article about the library, she was as
soft-spoken as the veritable church mouse, and made so little
impression on me that I had completely forgotten she existed by
the time I discovered she was involved in the Goodwin drama.

An excerpt from
Make Believe Love
by Jason Warwick

[Tuesday, June 13th]

You're just using me.

This is simply entertainment for you. Isn't it?
My life. You're using my life to escape from yours.
Whatever.

I'm tired. I don't have the slightest urge to go on. Could
I really tell you anything that would change your mind
about me? As usual, I'm deluding myself. You've seen me
on the news. The news doesn't lie.

So, this is all pointless, isn't it? I'm afraid so. I wish you
could convince me otherwise. The coffee certainly isn't
working this morning. I don't know. Could you show me a
sign or something?

I suppose not. You don't even exist yet. I mean, you're
out there somewhere, living a life so miserable you will one
day have need of mine for escape, but you are not yet aware
that somewhere on the edge of the world you've already
begun a relationship with a crazy woman.

Or maybe not.

Maybe you haven't even been born yet.

Imagine that. I'm dreaming you into being before sperm meets egg, perhaps even before your mother and father or your grandmothers and grandfathers have been born. I might as well be a god. Or perhaps it is you who are the god of my creation, the perfection of my love, pieced together out of all my accumulated mistakes and corrections.

All right. What the hell. We're practically halfway there anyway.

What have I got to lose?

Mom invited me out for lunch one day soon after the Warhol fiasco. Something in her voice warned me to stay away—she'd been pestering me to round up "some of my girlfriends" for one of her cosmetics parties (did I not mention that in her spare time she sells cosmetics for some sort of pyramid marketing scheme?)—but I'd been putting her off too long, so I accepted. She suggested Eric's. I hadn't been there since my interview and the place had that two hours of my life embedded in its plastic ferns and Arborite marble tabletops. I felt a bit dizzy thinking about Jason sitting across the table that day while I stared at Mom's new orange lips. They matched her dress, which, she proudly informed me, she'd made herself.

"It's very nice."

"I'll bet you sometimes wish you'd learned to sew, don't you?"

"Yes," I tried to nod solemnly, affecting the air of one who has glimpsed the error of her life's chosen course. "I spend hours every day regretting my lack of sewing skills. And my inability to kiss ass."

She frowned deeply and began fidgeting with the narrow black collar of her original Swiftian design.

"You know I hate to hear you use that sort of language. Why do you always have to be so sarcastic?"

"Sorry."

"I ask you a simple question and suddenly I'm being attacked."

"I said I was sorry."

She leaned across the table and patted my hand.

"Apology accepted."

She'd tried to teach me to sew, tempting me with a complete wardrobe of doll clothes, but I had no natural ability: every pin wanted my blood and I'd end up hurling my Frankensteinian creations across the room and nursing my poor appendages. Just one more way I'd disappointed her.

She ordered a tossed salad and a cup of coffee.

"Trying to lose some weight," she whispered across the table in an obscenely cute and conspiratorial way, as though we were sisters or something, and all a sudden I felt like throwing up. There was a man. I suppose I should have expected this, but it had never occurred to me, and now it suddenly became appallingly clear that my mother was dating. Or at least that was her plan: my mother wanted to invite some stranger up to her condominium for some mutual tonguing and stroking after an evening of wining and dining.

"Are you okay?"

"No. I don't ... I don't feel well."

"Oh, honey. What is it? Your stomach?"

"Yes."

"Is it a flu? Have you seen a doctor?"

"No, it's all right. I'll be okay. I just don't feel like eating."
She leaned in close again.
"You're not … pregnant?"
"No!"
For a moment she stared self-consciously at the table, then started talking about Dr. Doidge, her boss, and his latest bad habit: humming Céline Dion while he shone his little light into patients' pupils. I picked up my fork and studied it, trying to define the exact point where one tine became another, imagining what my mother would do if I were to drive it into the centre of my own forehead. Would it actually stick there, in my skull? That would take a great deal of force. The skull is not so easily invaded. It's a lonely prison, and no one gets out alive. I considered voicing these platitudes, but decided against it. She'd only accuse me of being unladylike. She was always accusing me of being unladylike.

"So that was something, Broken Head making the national news—wasn't it? I told you that man is dangerous."

"He's dangerous to overpriced wallpaper."

"Oh, you're an art critic now? Well, I have to agree with you, I really didn't see the beauty in it, but I think that that's beside the point in this instance. You did call the police, didn't you? You know if he starts on you, you'll need that record. There'd be nothing you could do to talk him out of it. You know he believes that Stephanie Rush sends him messages."

"Maybe she does. Maybe she talks to him out of a screen."

"No. In the trees. Something about messages in the trees he plants around his farm."

Mother chattered on, working herself up to what she really wanted to say, which she'd managed to do by the time the salad appeared.

"How many classes are you taking this term?"

"Anthropology and English."

These were night courses at the regional college. I was pasting together a degree in my spare time, taking whatever was available in the way of electives, still with no clear idea of what I wanted to be if I grew up. My brother Brian was in engineering in Saskatoon and I suspected Mom was lending him money, though Brian denied it. She had a pretty good job as Dr. Doidge's receptionist, something she'd taken up about ten years before to help subsidize the farm. For my birthday she'd given me some baby powder, the usual makeover kit, and a hundred-dollar bill inside a card ornate with birds and flowers and ribbons. I used it to pay for my birth control prescription.

"Why don't you move to Saskatoon and go to school full time? Brian's roommate had a nervous breakdown and moved back home. You could live with him."

"With Brian's neurotic roommate? Sounds interesting."

She ignored me.

"*Brian* needs someone to split the rent. He'd be happy to have you. You could still get registered. I checked."

I set the fork down.

"Really? Brian wouldn't mind living with me? He said that?"

"Well.... No. I haven't asked him, yet. But he's always complaining about money."

"Brian and I would kill each other in a week."

"Oh, I'm sure you've both matured enough to manage to get along. It would be good for you."

She was paying too much attention to her salad, picking away at an elusive olive, refusing to meet my eyes.

"I can't afford to go to school full time. I can't quit my job."

"I can lend you some money, dear."

The orange lips smiled graciously.

"Thanks." I finally responded, completely chastened by her generosity. "But I can't, Mom. I can't possibly live with Brian."

She sighed in exasperation. "So the two of you are going to throw separate dollars away on rent. Fine. I'm sure you can find another roommate. But it would mean a lot to me if you could watch out for him, Joan. His marks aren't what they should be. I think he's partying too much instead of applying himself."

She set down her fork and began fiddling with her dress again, wiping at it with a napkin to erase a tiny drop of oil that had spattered on the breast of her jacket. I'd been trying to place the inspiration for her black collar and it finally came to me: all the female anchorwomen were wearing them.

"I'm not going to Saskatoon, Mom. I have no desire to look after my little brother. I've got my own life right now, and I'm happy. And anyway, I need to stay here."

"Why?" she challenged me, still dabbing at the damned spot with her napkin.

"I'm worried about Dad."

This was my own challenge, and she wasted no time in taking it up.

"I think your father's old enough to take care of himself."

"So am I, Mom. I'm not a little girl. I'm all grown up."

And now she forgot her dress and eyed me in a way

that said she had me where she wanted me—that I'd stupidly wandered defenceless into her sights with such a preposterous claim.

"Oh, you are, are you? Then why are you having an affair with Jason Warwick?"

I couldn't think of what else to do, so I stood up to leave. Half a dozen people at the surrounding tables were glancing at us, whispering, doing everything but pointing.

"Joan! Think about what you're doing to yourself."

I had to get back at her. I had to hurt her.

"You're jealous, aren't you? You're jealous because you don't know *how* to love."

Her full lips became almost surreal in their orangeness when contrasted against the awful colour her face was turning, and she was shaking so visibly it seemed possible she might actually explode; she began to hiss something very very quietly, but, unfortunately, not quietly enough that I couldn't make out the words.

"Your behaviour disssgussstsss me. Don't bother calling me again until you've broken it off."

I didn't point out that she was the one who had called me. Instead, I told her, "If I'd known screwing a married man would get me out of talking to you, I'd have done it years ago."

I stormed away, past all those carefully averted faces. Or maybe they never really were eavesdropping. Maybe they hadn't heard anything at all. Still, I was tempted to take a bow.

Dad was disgusted too. Not that he said anything. He stopped calling, stopped accepting my supper invitations.

When I dropped in on him in his dismal little apartment he made an excuse about how he had no time for me.

"Studying," he said.

Our little house looked like the Taj Mahal next to his place: a ten-by-twelve room with a hot plate, sink and bar-sized fridge in the corner, paisley wallpaper peeling at the ceiling, a yellowed 1933 newspaper visible underneath. He slept on a cot that he rolled into the closet in the daytime. There was the smell of something I couldn't identify—it might have been mould or rat droppings in the walls or it might have been a cure for cancer in his fridge or it might have been whisky on his breath that he'd tried to mask by brushing his teeth. If so, he'd hidden the bottle somewhere.

"I've got a big exam coming up."

He was taking courses at the college, too, pursuing the papers that would testify to the fact he could do heavy-duty mechanics. Before I left I tried to hug him, but he only put one arm around me and patted my back half-heartedly. When I stepped away he looked at me as though I had hurt and shamed him more than anyone ever had. I tried to meet his eyes, but he looked away.

I stopped inviting him for dinner.

Before long, it seemed the only person in town who didn't know was Carol MacAndrew. Jason intimated that she knew there was someone, that she had her own liaisons, that he only wanted us to maintain discretion for the sake of appearances and so as not to rub her nose in it. I was never sure whether it was true. But I willingly suspended my disbelief.

She was a peroxide blonde who tried her best to simulate the same aura of sophistication as Jason did, but you could smell Broken Head on her. I remember one winter day when she walked up to my counter with two books to check out: *Obsessive Love: When Passion Holds You Prisoner* and *Finding Intimacy*. She smiled politely. The pearls decorating her distended lobes matched her white parka, white dress, white stockings and shoes.

"Nice day," I said, though it was minus thirty-two outside, and she nodded absently, staring out the window at the bank of snow heaped around the perimeter of the parking lot, shining like a dying star in the afternoon sun. A pair of sunglasses with ivory frames was perched on top of her head and she lowered them over her eyes before she turned to pick up her books.

"Thank you," she said, and sashayed out the door, where she disappeared instantly, like a polar bear slipping into a blizzard.

That happened after I'd told Jason that I never wanted to see him again. It was not the first time I'd met Carol. Months earlier I'd gone to her office, pretending I wanted to buy a house, and she drove me out to look at one in my range.

"I love your earrings," she chirped, quite a different person when we were on her professional ground and there was the possibility of selling me something. "I have a set of pearls that my grandmother gave me and I cherish them more than anything else I own."

"These are fake."

She giggled nervously.

"Really? Well, they certainly look real. And that's all that matters, isn't it?"

I gave her one of my blank stares.

"Well, *I* think so. Why pay twice as much for something that doesn't look any better? Not that—I mean, quality and workmanship are important, of course."

"And nothing makes a pearl quite like a dedicated oyster." She laughed even more nervously.

"True. We really should think about the oyster, shouldn't we?" She paused for a moment, apparently thinking. "You know, I had never ever considered the oyster. They must just peel them open and rip those pearls out, I suppose?"

I shrugged.

"What else are oysters for?"

She squirmed. Right there in the driver's seat, she squirmed. There was something sexy about it: rubbing her bum into the velour that way. And that made me think of Jason and her. And that made me bite my tongue hard and look out the side window at the rows of sad bungalows filing past.

"I suppose the oyster wouldn't look at it that way, though?" she asked, trying to sound apologetic.

I didn't bother responding. When the silence got too long I wondered if I should mention that I knew her brother. I had told her that I'd lived in Broken Head all my life but, strangely, she hadn't pursued it as I'd expected; hadn't sought out that connection that might help her make the sale.

Before I could say anything we pulled into a driveway and she motioned through the windshield at a green double garage door that was apparently hiding a home. "I think you'll like this place. It's a perfect starter for a new family."

I'd told her I was engaged. I'd explained that my intended couldn't be there because he was working. She led me up the front steps, briskly motioned me inside, and began giving me the Cook's tour, recovering her composure now that she could shift into this familiar role.

"And this is one of the smaller bedrooms. Are you planning on children?"

"Oh, yes, definitely. We're having a whole brood. Five or six, I hope." I admired the wallpaper printed with Teddy Bears floating off into cotton candy clouds on bunches of rainbow-coloured balloons. "I just love kids."

"Isn't that wonderful. They really are the greatest gift this life has to offer."

She took a step toward the door.

"You have children?"

She paused in the doorway, but she couldn't look at me when she answered.

"No. Not yet. The career thing, you know?" She brought her hand up and swept a lock of her plastic hair behind her ear. "Let me show you the master bedroom."

I already knew the master bedroom. I'd fucked her husband there the week before.

There was something transcendent about coupling in those strange rooms. They had the mark of domesticity about them, of other people's *be*ing, people I could imagine in secure happy marriages in secure happy lives. What we were committing was an intimate occupation of those imagined happy lives, shedding our own identities a little every time we undressed and tried our best to share our skins. That was the important thing, to become unrooted, to open up the possibilities of existence so wide that all the limitations of self were eliminated entirely. Call it madness if you like; if that is your only way of interpreting ecstasy.

Perhaps all I'm really talking about is orgasm. Real toe-clenching, spine-arching, earth-shattering orgasm. I had never experienced that particular quality of euphoria before. And at first, orgasm was enough. I'd convinced myself that I didn't believe in love anyway. Love was just a cheap romantic notion invented to make sanctimonious people feel pure about fucking. What I'd found was perfect, even if you couldn't talk about it to anyone in the town where I lived. I had fine and simple sex with a guy who was old enough to know what he was doing, and young enough to be attractive; a guy who expected nothing from me except relief from the boredom of his relationship. There wasn't even anything morally wrong with what I was doing. I was only helping a couple out of a jam.

Good moral uncomplicated sex. What more could a young woman ask for?

The only problem was, sometimes I couldn't quite put him properly out of my head, even when I needed to. I would walk by his house two or sometimes three times a day, just on the chance that he might emerge as I was strolling by, but at the same time I worried that he would indeed see me and think that I was spying on him, so that once or twice when I did spot him emerging with the lawn-mower or on his way somewhere, I turned and hurried off in the other direction.

And I went twice more to look at houses with Carol. Playing the young wife and mother-to-be. Watching her. Wondering what it was about her that had attracted him. Was it the same thing he saw in me? Was I just another version of her—the small-town girl, but seen from an entirely different perspective? And that made me worry that I wasn't even as interesting as she had been when they'd met: the exotic innocent lost in the city.

Toronto. Big town on a Great dirty Lake. Centre of the Canadian universe. Or so Torontonians think. You can't really blame them. We all have the tendency to believe we're the centre of the universe, and the constant reassurance of the media that you are correct in thinking so would make it difficult to see the inanity of this position. One of the advantages of coming from Saskatchewan is you soon find it impossible to support the delusion that you are at the centre of anything.

How did I know Toronto? I had watched it on television all of my life. Toronto was a bland place where two-dimensional people spoke lifeless words that seemed to embarrass them, but somehow they couldn't quite stop themselves from uttering. And then there were the commercials. That's where Toronto was truly exciting: in the beer ads. Lots of cute and mindless twenty-something boys, and the women … well, we won't even talk about the women.

The real city was a pleasant surprise. I met Jason there that September, only a month after Goodwin painted his Warhol. Jason had left Carol behind with the excuse that he needed to visit his father. There was no question that Carol might want to come: she hated his father almost as much as his father hated her.

Our room was on the twenty-eighth floor of a downtown hotel that was sufficiently posh to impress me. I have one particularly vivid memory of a young man bringing in room service while I lay sprawled under the covers, luxuriously naked, watching him try his best to steal furtive glances at me without my noticing. I felt like a queen, or at least like the king's mistress. Jason, clad in his hotel-issue white terry bathrobe, handed the boy a five and sent him on his way.

The weather was sublime sunshine, while back home the farmers were worried about snow.

I had fun. There was plenty of shopping. One afternoon we caught the ferry to Centre Island and walked, dodging bicyclers and rollerbladers, feeling thankful we had escaped the beggars and the mentally ill. We went on the Ferris wheel and when we reached the top of our orbit he kissed me and whispered some silly verse of Byron's in my ear.

He took me to the cool clubs and quirky restaurants he had once frequented, sometimes discovering them closed or empty or attempting some kind of reinvention because they were no longer cool or quirky enough, and even in those places that had remained popular he would complain about how their standards had slipped—that nothing was as fine as it was when he was the young lion who ruled this town.

Men or women, former acquaintances, would sometimes approach our table, and Jason would have short comic conversations about having discovered hell on earth, assuring them that it would not be long before he returned, though he couldn't say exactly when. After discussing his Goodwin photos, which they'd all seen but most did not know their old friend was responsible for, Jason would emphasize the amount of writing he was doing, portraying his job at the *Standard* as a research project he was carrying out for the sake of a novel he would one day write—a novel that was presumably about a small-town journalist who moved to the city and lost his naive innocence when faced with the complexities of the real world. Sometimes he would introduce me as a friend; sometimes, if it didn't seem necessary, he wouldn't bother to introduce me at all.

No one asked about Carol.

One day, when he was visiting with his closest friends, I saw three movies in an afternoon.

On the last day, we actually did visit his father, and the grand old man got a bit deep in his cups, as he himself put it, and ended up propositioning me.

"You're a lovely woman. A very lovely woman. I can't believe you sprung from the same foul hole that spawned this young dilettante's horrible, white-trash, *nouveau riche* sugar mama. Why are you wasting your time with him? He's attached. And look at him! He's hopelessly superficial. All flash. Not a spark of depth. You could have anyone you want. You could have me."

He swept his hand across his gabardine jacket in a flourish, trying to mimic a maître d' signifying his offering. He was quite distinguished-looking and wasn't *that* old: maybe fifty-five.

"Why, thank you," I said, as demurely as I could manage, and took a sip of my Cosmopolitan.

"Shut up, Dad," was all Jason could think to respond. We were on a patio on Queen Street, watching and being watched by the hordes of pedestrians swarming by.

"He's a liar, too. A compulsive liar. Nay, a pathological liar!"

"The pot calling the kettle black," Jason said, his voice almost completely lost in the clatter of a street car squealing past. His father stretched his arms and flapped them, casting off this insult before it could take root.

"Let me tell you a little secret, my dear. After his mother ran off with that janitor—"

"You mean, after she caught you sleeping with one of your first-year students," Jason interrupted him.

"Oh, yes. The moral arbiter is scolding me for the benefit of his mistress. No offence intended to you, my dear. I consider 'mistress' to be a most noble calling." He touched my arm. "After he started going to school out in the darkest depths of Mississauga, his mother discovered he was telling all of his new friends that his father was a dead war hero. Or was it that he'd died in a fire, trying to save a baby from a burning building?"

"Bullshit," Jason said.

"Entirely," his father said.

I tried, a bit desperately, to bridge the gap.

"But isn't that—wasn't it kind of nice that he said those things about you?"

Those hands of his would not stop moving, and now one of them ended up on my knee.

"Somehow, my dear, I don't think he was talking about me. I think he was talking about the daring man of action he wished he'd had for a father."

"Shut up, Dad!" Jason said violently enough to make the couple at the next table turn and stare.

"That's the way he always speaks to his father. Can a man be trusted if he speaks to his father that way?"

The hand had moved on from my knee by now, and was being employed to punctuate this speech to the neighbouring couple. They turned away and fingered their drinks, smirking with embarrassment for us. Two young professionals dressed all in black, nurturing or closing some sort of deal, by the look of it. Business is relationships. Perhaps they were even conducting their own affair but, if so, they hadn't invited their father along.

"Please, Dad," Jason whispered. "Try to behave yourself."

"I suppose he's still pretending to be a writer, is he?"

I laughed nervously. He ploughed on.

"All I've ever asked is that he use a pseudonym, but he refuses. My greatest fear is that some day he'll actually publish some of his drivel in a venue where someone might actually read him, and my professional name will be forever ruined, or at least horribly stained for a season before the hideous tome slips from the shelves. 'How could you have encouraged him?' they'll ask me. And I will bear up and face it with my best profile. I'll say 'I think his work is promising, actually. It may translate into a decent movie. Or, more likely, an indecent one.'"

I thought Jason might ignite into actual physical violence, but exactly the opposite happened. Shrunk in his chair, he seemed to have become a small boy, and when he turned and met my pitying eyes, I felt as though I were becoming his mother. "Yes, Dad's always been very supportive," he said, smiling weakly.

"She's a beautiful woman. You don't deserve her," his father told him, then lifted his empty martini glass and rolled the olive into his mouth.

"You're absolutely right." Jason raised his glass to salute me.

His father spat the olive pit into his hand and placed it on the table before me, a small token of his appreciation.

"I wouldn't trust him as far as I could throw him," he said, and motioned to the pit. I picked it up and tossed it out into the traffic, where it skipped once before disappearing under the rushing wheels of a Volkswagen. Mr. Warwick smiled broadly. "A good arm. And other good parts, too."

Afterwards, I was more than a little surprised at how pleased Jason seemed to be with the whole visit, as if everything had gone perfectly. "Oh, he's just being Dad," was all he'd say when I attempted to express my sympathy.

We made love, for what might have been the last time, in the shower of our hotel room, the water pulsing in my face, so that when I opened my mouth to gasp for air I almost drowned.

I was welcomed back to Broken Head by Susie threatening to move out.

"It's just ... I don't know. I don't think you're who I thought you were."

"Really? Who am I?"

I handed her a plate. We were doing the dishes when she'd finally screwed herself up to dropping this bombshell.

"I don't know. I don't think this ... arrangement is working any longer."

"Really? What's not working about it?"

"I just don't feel I can count on you as a friend any more."

She couldn't look at me.

"Really? And that was part of the deal?"

"I thought it was."

I slammed on the hot water to rinse and caught a breath of the rising steam.

"Oh. Sorry. I understood we were splitting the rent on a house."

Susie began wiping her eyes with her dishtowel.

"Well, I thought we were friends. I thought you were my best friend. It's not like I'm in love with you or anything, but I thought we were good friends."

"And what exactly have I done to betray our wonderful friendship?"

She had dissolved further into her dishtowel.

"You don't ... you don't ... you don't tell me your secrets. You don't tell me where you go when you go for your walks. You don't tell me how you could suddenly afford to go for holidays in Vancouver for a week."

Saying these words made her more and more frantic with grief, so that by the time she'd finished speaking she was sucking in air and wailing like a newborn with its first handprint on its poor little bum. I stood there, soaking my fingers in the suds, mesmerized by her despair, wondering how I could have aroused such passionate emotions in anyone. Would Jason cry for my secrets?

"My secret?" I murmured when she'd begun to get control of herself. She peered at me over the edge of her limp dishrag. "You want to know my secret? I'm in love with a married man."

It was as though I'd handed her a bouquet of exotic flowers.

"Oh, my God, it's true. Mom told me, but I didn't want to believe her."

"I actually hadn't discussed it with your mother."

"She heard a rumour," Susie said.

Which explained why Susie was thinking about moving out. Her parents were probably concerned about my influence and had told her it would be better if she came home. I don't say this to be snide: I like Susie's parents. She was an only child, and it was obvious they loved her very much and were always concerned about her well-being—had even been grateful when I took her under my wing. Her mother had confided in me that she felt it was about time Susie got out and discovered the world.

"If your mother knows, everybody in town knows."

"Not necessarily," Susie tried to reassure me. "Mom hears things that not everybody ..."

"I wasn't really in Vancouver. I was in Toronto. With him. The bastard was so ashamed of me he wouldn't even introduce me to his friends. He did introduce me to his father. His father made a pass at me. I broke it off on the last day. I told him I never wanted to see him again."

"Oh, Joan, honey," Susie said, and rushed to comfort me by wrapping her arms around me and bawling into my shoulder. And, much to my surprise, I found that I was weeping too. I tried to stop myself, but the grief came from somewhere deep, and now that it had coursed its way to the surface there was no holding it back. I wept not for myself, but for Susie, who was weeping for me—despicable me. And I wept for Carol MacAndrew. I did. And I wept for Laurie Johnson and her parents. And I wept for my father. And I wept for my mother. And finally, when all of my tears were gone and Susie still went on weeping, I held her head to my shoulder and imagined that I had just told Jason that I loved him but I did not believe that he could ever love me and that he was weeping into my shoulder until the silk of my blouse clung to my skin.

The truth works in strange ways. On the surface, I suppose I lied to Susie when I told her I'd already dumped Jason, but to all intents and purposes the words became true the moment I spoke them. I can't claim to have known for sure that I would dump him until I spoke, but once the words were out of my mouth there was no longer any doubt. It was over.

The only problem was that it began to seem Jason had already discarded *me* without bothering to let me know. He didn't call for over six weeks after Toronto. I considered calling him at home or at work and arranging a meeting myself—burying him over the phone would just be too cruel—though this had been strictly forbidden. I would have done it, too, except that I was worried he'd simply hang up on me, and the click of the receiver would be my only confirmation that I was no longer desirable.

I took to walking by his work, as it wasn't so impossible that I might have just been happening to walk by on my way to the drug store or the liquor store or the grocery store or the post office. I never so much as glanced through the plate glass windows. I wanted him to see me but I didn't want him to see me trying to see him.

Meanwhile, Susie, ever supportive of my brave move, took to attacking Jason as her favourite sport.

"You see that photograph of Darwin Goodwin spray-painting was on the cover of a tabloid?"

I nodded. "*The World Weekly Exhaust*, wasn't it?"

"What would he have done if Goodwin had said he was going to kill someone? Would he have set up a tripod and waited?"

"Oh, likely. He probably would have offered to bring along the murder weapon. He probably would have sold tickets."

If I was good enough to play along with her she'd usually let it drop, but sometimes I couldn't help but be disagreeable.

"Well, say what you like, but he saved *our* jobs."

"What! What are you talking about?"

We were in the living room, surrounded by her ever expanding herd of penguins, me slouched on the couch, Susie sprawled on the floor in front of the television.

"There wouldn't be a library if it wasn't for him."

"Oh, fidget." That was as close as Susie ever got to swearing. "The people of Broken Head saved my job. Mrs. White saved my job. The mayor wouldn't do anything that ticked off Mrs. White, because she'd make sure it would tick off Mr. White." The Whites had made a fortune in the oil industry. "All he did was write a couple of articles. He was doing his job."

"Exactly. You think the old *Standard* reporter would've subjected himself to library board meetings?"

I told her what Jason's source had told him about the secret library board meeting: how the mayor demanded to know if the grille in the middle of the ceiling was a bug, and when the chairman told him he believed it was for ventilation, he ordered someone from Public Works be called in to remove the grille for inspection.

"If he weren't rich, he'd be committed."

"Maybe so," Susie said. "I'm not saying that the mayor's not nuts. I'm saying that Jason *War*wick never saved *my* job."

"He did more than you or I did," I said, standing to throw the cushions off the couch, thereby giving the signal that it was time for Susie to retreat to her bedroom. "He did more than *us*, even though we work there."

She rose to her feet and began to sulk off to her room, only to pause, balance on one leg, the way she had a habit of doing when she became particularly self-conscious—taking a stork's stand—and ask, "Why do you defend him?"

"I'm not defending him," I said. "I'm just pointing out that he has his good points. He's not Count Dracula."

Susie scuttled away, closed her door behind her, and didn't open it again until the next afternoon. By that time, I'd already left for my Sunday shift at the library.

The following Sunday was Susie's shift, and Jason must have still been keeping track, because I'd just slid into my afternoon bath when the phone rang. I managed to scramble to it, dripping water everywhere, before the machine picked up.

"Guess who," he said.

"Count Dracula?"

In the moment's silence before he responded I could hear traffic noises. He must have been on his way to the corner for milk or something, and had stopped at some secluded payphone. I was crouched on the floor. The curtains were all open and I didn't even have a towel.

"Sorry it's been so long. Life's been … a little crazy."

"Tell me about it."

"I want to see you."

"Sure. I'll be right over. Tell Carol to put on the kettle."

A car without a muffler chugged by in the background.

"Listen, I can't talk long. Tomorrow night. I'll pick you up at the park."

The chugging faded. I hugged my knees for warmth. We kept the thermostat turned down to save money.

"You have to rush. Carol is awaiting the milk. Or is it eggs for a cake she's baking? Angel food, no doubt."

"What exactly is your problem? Oh, shit. Here comes Mrs. Horne." Mrs. Horne was one of Carol's mother's best friends. "I'm just giving her the smile and the sweet wave. Fucking town."

"Say hello to her from me."

He sighed heavily.

"I gotta go. Will you meet me?"

"I'll be there," I said.

He tried to slam down the receiver and missed, so that I heard it fall, and listened to it dangling there, spinning, before he snatched it up and whacked it into its cradle.

In the end, I must have spent almost as much time with the clerk at the EasyMart, watching her scan my butter and eggs, as I spent with Jason over the course of that spring, summer, and fall. Our last meeting was on the seventh of November. It was already dark when he picked me up at a corner by the park about three blocks from home. He was ten minutes late. My toes were freezing and I'd taken off my gloves to rub the circulation back into my ears, but when I pulled open the car door and dropped into the passenger seat, it was he who started complaining.

"Jesus, this weather. How do people stand it? I mean, why the fuck would anyone *live* here?"

"We're tough," I said, too cold to be more ingenious. My tone made him back off a bit.

"You work today?"

"Yes."

He was silent a while and I thought he was trying to think of something else to talk about.

"Does Goodwin ever show up looking for you?"

"No. He's in jail. Remember?"

"He's out on bail. But come to think of it, one of the conditions is that he can't go near the library."

"Oh, that must be why then. He drives past my house every day at six."

"Seriously!"

"No, not seriously."

We pulled up to a stop sign and he began tapping his fingers on the wheel.

"I wish *you* wouldn't walk by my house so often."

"What do you mean, 'often'?"

"Aren't you worried Carol'll notice?"

"You really think a lot of yourself, don't you? I walk where I walk and my walking has nothing to do with you."

"You've got quite a chip on your shoulder, haven't you? I'm sorry it's been so long, but I've been very busy."

"It doesn't matter. After tonight you won't have to worry about making time for me."

He turned and looked at me.

"What do you mean?"

"I've had enough. I don't want to do this any more."

My plan was that this would lead to a heated battle where I could say all that I wanted to say to him, but instead the light turned green and he pushed his foot down on the accelerator to express his anger, and the dark gods must have pricked up their ears. Up ahead I saw a car stop at a side street, then begin to pull out in front of us.

"Jason!"

He jammed on the brakes.

There wouldn't have been a chance, even if he'd been driving below the speed limit. The other driver hadn't even looked. It really wasn't entirely our fault. We weren't going that fast.

The moment before impact slowed down in the way those moments always do. My hands were braced on the dashboard. I could see the other driver's face, an old woman, impossibly old, blue hair tied into a silk scarf, her mouth opening as she looked straight into my eyes.

The impact itself seemed unnaturally light, as if perhaps we had somehow simply passed through the car, our molecules dividing to prevent such meaningless violence. When our car had stopped skidding and come to a rest against the curb, I turned to Jason. He sat silent for a few seconds, a vein beside his eye pulsing the way it sometimes did when we made love, his hands still gripping the wheel.

"This *fucking* town. Doesn't anyone know how to drive in this *fucking* town?"

He threw open the door.

"Stay here!"

I thought he was maybe off to beat the woman senseless as punishment for her stupidity. She was so old and frail that I thought it best if I jumped out to defend her, but my intentions were immediately halted when I saw the extent of the damage. The driver's side was crumpled in from where we had glanced before her car skipped away like a billiard ball. Jason stood staring in her shattered window. He tried yanking open the back door, but no matter how he struggled it would not give. I began to approach and he whirled around and saw me. His face was pale, but when he registered my face he started yelling.

"Get out of here! Just walk!"

I stopped, stood there staring at him.

"Get away! The cops'll be coming."

And so I turned and ran.

I heard about the accident the next day at work. Susie's mother often called her with the latest gossip, and she'd cradle the phone between her ear and her shoulder and take it in while she sorted through the overdues. That day, when she got off the phone she came rushing breathlessly over to me and said, "Jason Warwick killed Vanessa Walsh's grandmother."

I did not respond. I can only imagine what my face registered, but Susie quickly added, "Well, he hit her with his car anyway. Hit her car. And the police are pressing charges."

"Oh," I said.

"Or, at least, that's what Mom heard. He hadn't been drinking or anything, but he *was* speeding. You know that new Mercedes of his? Totalled."

I nodded grimly, resisting the temptation to tell her that it was a BMW.

"At least, that's what Mom heard. It was icy, though. And the Walshes had been trying to convince her she shouldn't be driving. She wasn't … as sharp as she used to be."

"No," I said. At that moment a man came to the counter and I stood up and checked out his books. When I was finished, Susie was still hovering.

"Vanessa Walsh's grandmother," I said, and Susie nodded, then returned to her overdues.

In the end they did not press charges. As it turned out, Mrs. Walsh was in the early stages of Alzheimer's, and when that was combined with the icy conditions and the fact that Jason's skid marks had been marred by footprints and the tire tracks of other cars, they were far beyond a reasonable doubt.

Susie's mother was going to the funeral, and Susie decided to tag along. She tried to convince me to come, but I told her I didn't know the woman and didn't feel right about it, hinting that maybe she should feel the same, but she didn't take the bait. I was watching television when she came home, and she stood in the doorway, stamping her boots, positively glowing, as though she'd come from a wedding.

"Oh, I wish you'd been there. It was a lovely service. They left an open mike and people got up to speak about her. You wouldn't believe how many lives she touched."

"Uh-huh," I said, switching channels.

Dad started coming over for supper again.

I went out twice with a fellow in my Human Justice class, but his only passion was for Garth Brooks and he had breath that didn't quite stink, but made me concerned about what exactly it was he was eating.

Mom called and asked me if I could get my girlfriends together for a cosmetics party. I told her I was too busy right now, and I didn't have that many girlfriends anyway, but that we should get together for dinner sometime soon.

I promised myself never to walk by Jason's house again, and to sharpen my resolve I started inviting Susie along for my strolls, and we would stretch our legs the fourteen blocks to the video store and back, and then Susie would make popcorn while I confirmed how dismal the television fare actually was.

Another day at work Susie came rushing up and spread out a yellowed newspaper on the counter before me.

"Look at this! Is this man related to you?"

It was a copy of *The Broken Head Standard* from 1947 that she'd dug from the archival material stacked up in paper file boxes in the storage room. She was pointing out a story on the second page about Abraham Froese and how, in the midst of seeding his wheat, he'd found a wallet with fifteen dollars cash in it lying in his field. It belonged to a neighbour, Matthew Swift, who had lost it six months before.

"He was my grandfather. He died before I was born."

"Really? Freaky! Look at this."

She pointed out a story in the next column, describing how relatives from British Columbia had spent a few days visiting the Alford family on their way through Broken Head.

"So?"

"Alford was Evvy Walsh's maiden name."

"Evvy Walsh?"

"Vanessa's grandmother. That was her family. Her father's brother lost his farm in the Depression and moved to B.C. He was visiting them."

I waited for Susie to supply the punchline. She stood there staring at me.

"And …?" I finally said.

"Well … isn't it neat? Your grandfather and Evvy Walsh on the same page of the newspaper."

I went back to unloading the book bin.

"That's really something, Susie."

"Yeah! It's like … your grandfather and Mrs. Walsh are connected somehow."

"Oh, yes, connected. They're practically soulmates."

Susie watched me Dewey-decimalling the books for a few silent moments before she finally folded up the newspaper.

"I just thought you might be interested."

A week later she brought home a box of papers and ceremoniously dumped them out on our kitchen table. I was in the middle of cooking myself a grilled cheese sandwich.

"What's all this?"

"Guess."

"They're love letters from my grandfather to Evvy Walsh."

"No. They're Mrs. Walsh's papers. I offered to write a little history of her for the family. She was a remarkable woman."

She had already begun reading a long thin strip of paper, which looked like a grocery store receipt.

"You mean collecting penguins isn't satisfying you any more? I didn't realize you were so interested in history."

"There's a lot of things you don't realize about me."

I flipped my sandwich.

"This sudden interest in Mrs. Walsh wouldn't have anything to do with Jason Warwick, would it? Because, you know, I'd just as soon not be reminded of the existence of Jason Warwick."

She glanced up from her reading.

"Not everything has to do with you, Joan."

I started taking walks on my own again.

I began to wonder about the nature of history. How one event can cause another seemingly unrelated event, and, therefore, how the entire course of human history might have been altered. Human history. Inhuman history. And then there were all of those researchers and their documents, establishing the facts of who had been where and what they had done and how their actions had caused fluctuations in tea prices in China. Could the documents be misleading? If so, then the whole course of human history as we know it was thrown into question. And if we could not know the past, then how could we know ourselves? The documents had to be relied upon.

So if you were left out of a document, did that mean you were no longer culpable?

But, if that were the case, if one could be so easily absolved, did that mean that you ceased to exist in some small part of what would have otherwise been your life?

Did that part of you just die and wither away?

The twenty-second of February: the date proclaimed Thinking Day by Lord Baden Powell. I always thought of my mother on Thinking Day, because it had been her who'd forced me to stay in Girl Guides even when my friends were making fun of me in my uniform. I called her that morning and we talked in cautious tones about the distant possibility of spring, agreeing finally that I would go to her place for supper that evening. She told me to invite Susie as well. I said that she was working right now, and I thought she was going for supper with her own parents. I lied.

Jason called me later the same day. There was none of that awkward fumbling for connection. We both carried on as though the break had never happened. He spent most of the conversation complaining about his editor's fondness for stories about pets. I remember giggling like a high-school coquette. His voice sounded deeper, wiser, than it had three months before, as though something important had been revealed to him since the last time I faced him and he told me to run.

The housing market was dead in winter and our tracks in the snow on a walk might have raised Carol's suspicions, but I'd already been imagining a place we might go to if he ever called me again.

Insurance had replaced his car with a replica so exact that I couldn't tell the difference. We drove out to the abandoned farm where I was raised. There, parked in the yard, the engine running and the heater blowing, we made love in the passenger seat. It was cramped, but he was there with me, and I don't mean just holding me and physically inside me, but with me in his eyes and in his brain. I excited him. In my only attempt at intimacy with the guy in Human Justice—I can't even remember his name any more—it had become obvious that he'd learned to make love while studying the pages of a magazine and didn't quite know how to go about it with anyone else in the room.

We drank a few pulls of Crown Royal Jason had smuggled along in a flask, and then we struggled back into our clothes and broke into the house. I took him from room to empty room, blithely running a commentary. When I saw he didn't appreciate me mimicking Carol, I instantly transformed myself into a museum guide.

"And if you look to the right you'll see the absolutely palatial picture window which once overlooked the spectacular Swift family dining-room table where the Swift family ate exquisite meals prepared by the loving hands of that culinary genius, Joan Swift."

"I can't believe you actually lived here. And not even that long ago," Jason said, running his finger through the dust on the windowsill. "Except for the awful yellow siding, it looks like it's been deserted for fifty years."

He rubbed the dust between his thumb and index finger, a sorcerer casting a spell.

"It's old. My grandfather grew up here."

"Why didn't we come here last summer? We could have brought a blanket or a couple of sleeping bags."

I shrugged.

"Never thought of it," I lied.

By the time we got to my bedroom it seemed that neither of us had anything to say and so we stood there searching the pink walls for some sign of me until we both became uneasy and ducked back through the doorway.

Jason wanted to leave right then, but I convinced him we should go for a tramp around the property. He was afraid to walk on the creek, citing the warnings that the *Standard* routinely ran about the menace of thin ice.

"Oh, you delicate flower, you. Don't believe everything you read. That only happens over rapids," I assured him, "and I know where all the rapids are. Besides, it's hardly ever deeper than two or three feet."

"That may be, but I'd still rather keep my feet on dry land."

"Oh, come on, city slicker. Live dangerously for once in your life."

But he wouldn't be convinced. To show him what a silly coward he was, I walked along the creek while he followed me on the bank, trying to persuade me that we'd gone far enough. How cruel of me. It might have been terrifying for him, waiting for me to be swallowed up and swept away by that terrible icy current he imagined just a fraction of an inch under my feet.

"Follow me, Jason Warwick," I teased him in my best evangelist's voice. "For veritably, I say unto you, if you have faith in me you too can walk on water."

When we got to the bridge I finally relented and climbed up the bank.

Before we left I showed him the barn. We climbed the wooden ladder to the mow and pulled the rope on its squeaky pulley to open the upper door. As we stood there looking into the moonlit yard I told him about my dream, my first memory, and he turned and peered into the darkness to where the beast might be hiding, waiting to make a final charge that would destroy us both.

A beast, or the ghost of my grandfather? Or the ghost of Evvy Walsh?

"Did he have big teeth?"

"I don't know. I never actually saw him. I just knew he was there. The way you know things in dreams."

He nodded, his face coming out of the shadows and into the moonlight as he turned to look into my eyes.

"Carol and I are in trouble," he said.

I started coughing. He watched me trying to get control of my throat.

"What do you … mean?" I finally managed to say.

"We're just … it just doesn't seem to work."

"Oh," I said.

"She says she's not so sure I really love her."

"How can you ever be sure of anything?"

He looked me in the eye.

"I don't know what to do. She's right. I have stopped loving her. I think I've fallen in love with you."

That word. It was the first time he'd ever actually said that word directly to me. I mean, he quoted it from his poems, but he'd never before spoken it himself. In his own words.

And then he touched me in a way meant to prove he loved me more than anything else on earth.

The touch, of course, cannot be documented.

Neither can the word.

On the drive back to town, as we slowed and turned at Goodwin's forest, Jason said, "A movie producer came to see me the other day. They're making a flick about Goodwin and Stephanie Rush. I guess the Warhol thing has everybody interested again. He wants me to interview Goodwin."

It was all very nonchalant, as though the thought had just popped into his head.

"But Goodwin won't talk to you," I said.

"Awww, you never know. He might. It's his chance to tell his side of the story."

"That never made any difference before."

"Not exactly true. There was what he did to the painting. That was a kind of a statement. He called me for that. And this is a big American television network. That kind of a platform could seduce him out of hiding."

"Do you really believe that?"

"Yeah."

"So have you called him?"

"Yeah."

"What'd he say?"

"He told me that his cows make less manure than I do, but that at least theirs is good for growing something." He shifted gears. "Sounds promising, doesn't it?"

I was silent for almost a minute, listening to the sound of

the gravel popping against the bottom of his car, waiting for him to ask, but all he added was: "I don't know. Maybe he'll come around."

"Do you want me to help?"

He turned to look at me, feigning surprise.

"No, it's too dangerous," he finally said.

"Why? He's never been violent."

"He tried to break into her mansion."

I tried to imagine this: the lovestruck suitor scaling the wall of her Hollywood home, trying to climb up the trellis, the moonlight in his eyes, the manure on the soles of his boots.

"He didn't want to hurt her."

"How do you know?"

"I know."

He didn't respond to this, seemed to accept my point as though I'd made it through some particularly compelling argument.

Broken Head was ten miles away in the bottom of a valley, but its lights loomed softly into the sky on the black horizon, a great warm halo enticing us into its glow. As if falling under its spell, Jason turned onto the highway and accelerated.

"You know what it is, don't you?" he asked.

"What *what* is?"

"You look a bit like her."

"Who?"

And he turned to me, the highway straight enough that he could have driven for ten minutes without looking away.

"Stephanie Rush."

He smiled. I didn't know what to say.

"Just a bit. Your eyes, I think. A little."

T hree weeks after Stephanie Rush was released from the Betty Ford Clinic, David Burke turned up on my icy doorstep, business card in hand. Burke was a successful vacuum cleaner salesman from Regina who had recently become a motion picture producer. He informed me that he was involved in the making of a television movie about the life of Stephanie Rush, centring principally on her victorious struggle with drug and alcohol abuse, but also touching on her relationship—or, rather, lack of relationship—with Darwin Andrew Goodwin. It was a co-production deal with the Fox network. The Saskatchewan Film Development Office had put up a hundred thousand dollars to hire a screenwriter from Hollywood to write the story. They did this with the proviso that much of the film would be shot in Saskatchewan. The writer, Powell Ellis, had never been to Saskatchewan or Alberta, but he'd seen photographs and concluded that the Canadian prairie wasn't much different from the Kansas he'd visited as a child on trips to his grandparents' farm—making an actual visit to either province completely unnecessary.

Mr. Burke's major problem, as he related it to me, was that while they did have the cooperation of Stephanie Rush, who was being handsomely compensated, Goodwin had refused to take part. In fact, he had threatened legal action, and had even gone so far as to chase Burke from his yard with a shotgun.

The conflation of terror and the stark prairie landscape had produced in Burke a feeling that he could only define as "sublime."

Burke claimed not to be concerned about Goodwin's legal threat, but only wished to achieve his cooperation for the sake of the story: though the film focused on Rush, Powell Ellis wanted more of Goodwin's perspective on events than he had been able to glean from the various court transcripts. Ellis hoped to show, through a finely tuned narrative, how Goodwin's pursuit of Rush had been one of the major factors leading to her substance abuse problem. For this reason, he felt it was crucially important "to get Goodwin right."

This was where I came in: Burke hoped that I might be able to supply an introduction to Goodwin, seeing that I had had dealings with him in the past. He offered me a list of prepared questions, and said that if I could get a cassette recording of Goodwin answering them, I would be paid handsomely. I informed Burke that I had no wish to trespass in Goodwin's yard and be chased out with a shotgun; that considering our past dealings he would probably use the shotgun on me; and *that, therefore, I would be unable to help him. After reiterating that if I changed my mind I should immediately call him, he reluctantly went on his way.*

He didn't give up, though, for a few days later Mr. Burke turned up some information about a young woman who was rumoured to have carried on a long-term relationship with Goodwin. The next morning he was back in Broken Head, on Joan Swift's doorstep.

A day later, Joan Swift was on my doorstep with a proposition for me.

An excerpt from
Make Believe Love
By Jason Warwick

[Wednesday, June 14th]

Most farmers mark their driveway with a sign identifying their little piece of the world. Dad had his name painted on the wooden guide bar of an antique mower he'd parked by the grid road. For obvious reasons, Goodwin didn't follow this practice. He had a birdhouse, with no name on it at all, in the shape of a red barn. His house wasn't visible from the road, hidden as it was by rows and rows of Scotch pines he'd planted in straight lines so they could be cultivated. My father had neglected watering and monthly tillings when he'd attempted to plant a windbreak on our farm, and consequently his saplings had withered away, unable to compete with the weeds. It's a dry country.

We'd had a snap thaw starting three days before and the ditches were running like rivers. As I walked up the driveway, the tape recorder an uncomfortable bulge at the centre of my back, I surprised a gaggle of domestic geese feeding on some grain that had spilled out onto the road, and they turned and hissed at me. I shooed them—hissing right back the way I'd always done with the geese on our farm—and they waddled away, still hissing and impotently flapping their clumsy wings. The first building I came upon was a bungalow like the ones built on the south side of Broken Head in the mid-seventies—like one of the ones Carol'd tried to sell me. It had unblemished baby-blue siding and a white picket fence bounding a landscaped yard. The flowerbeds had been turned with well-rotted manure the fall before. I rang the bell, but no one answered. The door was locked. That seemed strange. We'd never locked the door on the farm. I didn't usually lock our door in town, though I'd promised Susie I would try to remember.

For a moment I felt grateful and was about to leave. But what good would that do? I'd just have to come back again. I decided to investigate further: he might be out working in his shop. I couldn't see any other buildings yet, because there were so many trees. I did notice a telephone line running off the corner of the house, so I followed it. As I continued on deeper, tight-roping between puddles, his woods suddenly gave way to a clearing containing a traditional farmhouse like the one I'd grown up in, except without the yellow siding. I'd estimate it was built in the twenties. The place was in general disrepair—the porch looked as though it was about to collapse—and badly in need of a coat of paint. Behind the house there was a red barn (a larger version of his birdhouse), a steel quonset, and six steel grainbins gleaming in the afternoon sunshine. The farm machinery parked around the yard was all very old—antiques really, though it was obvious these machines were still being used. I felt I'd wandered through a time warp into the 1950s, and wondered if I'd ever be able to find my way back to the present.

I hazarded the rotten wooden steps up to the porch and knocked at the door. A moment later it was opened by an elderly woman. Her grey tufted hair reminded me of the bear on Susie's bed, which had managed to hold on to most of its stuffing through all the years since her birth. The woman's eyes, though, had nothing in common with the bear's hollow black beads. They passed over my body, seeming to scornfully dismiss me, but instead she said, "It's about time you got here. Come on in. The kettle's on," and she turned and disappeared into the house.

It seemed I was expected. I looked down at the scarred doorstep and decided that it would not be safe to cross.

"Is ... Mr. Goodwin home?"

She appeared again in the inside doorway, looking at me in a way that made me feel I'd probably just asked the stupidest and most impertinent question in the history of language.

"It's calving time. He's out checking the cows. Come on in."

I didn't know what else to do but obey.

Her kitchen was an enormous swath of checkered linoleum towered over by underwater blue walls. I pulled out a chair and sat down at a table that could have sat sixteen for dinner without too much elbow joggling. The tiny woman, shuffling between cupboards for tea and teapot, then back to the stove to add the water, made the room feel even larger. Her years hadn't slowed her down much: she gave the impression of a small whirlwind as she hovered toward me with the flowered china.

"I hope you drink Earl Grey. I haven't had pekoe in years. I like this better. Less bitter."

"That's … fine."

She poured the tea, set the pot between us, and lowered herself into the severe oak armchair at the head of the table. She was so short that the pot obstructed her view of me and she had to lean forward to push it aside.

"You're prettier in real life."

"Pardon?"

"Than your pictures. You're prettier in real life than you are in your pictures."

I coughed, nodded manically, and took a sip of my tea.

"Just your photographs, I mean. I've never seen your moving picture shows. I don't go to the moving picture shows and I don't watch them on television. Nothing much I want to see on there. All sex and … that kind of thing. The only thing I watch is 'Lawrence Welk.' They took it off the air a few years back, but Dandy bought me a dish so that we could get it again."

She swished her tea around and stared into the bottom of the cup, reading her own future. I peered into my own but saw only blank white porcelain through the weak brew.

"I spoze you get 'Lawrence Welk' down there in California."

For a moment I thought she meant I was in California right now, and for that moment I felt I might be, we were so far apart with that mammoth table between us.

"I'm not sure what he's told you," she continued, "but I don't think I'm being unreasonable."

She seemed to be waiting for a response.

"No, no. Not at all," I assured her.

"It's just that … this place is overrun by ghosts—his father's ghost and the ghost of Old Mrs. Gunderson and the ghost of their hired man who hanged himself in the basement and … all the rest of them. And with that new house being so big and empty, there's no reason we couldn't all of us live there together. Don't you think so?"

I placed my cup in the circle of roses on the saucer.

"I don't see why not."

A wave of bitterness crossed her face.

"That's very generous of you, considering it's his father's money he built it with. Do you know what I had to go without all these years so that his father could save up all that money? You couldn't imagine. You young people nowadays can't imagine going without. Nobody ever built a brand new house for me. This one was already here when his father bought the place from the Gundersons. Old Mrs. Gunderson'd been laid up sick in bed for over ten years, with Old Mr. Gunderson feeding her and wiping her behind when she dirtied herself, and not a stitch of cleaning had been done in all those years. You couldn't imagine what it looked like when I moved in here."

She stopped talking, glaring at me now.

"No. I doubt that I could."

"I had to scrape the floor with a putty knife to get the dirt off. The walls were all so thick with dust they had to be washed and then repainted. There's nothing dirtier than a man. I'd say they're like pigs, but that wouldn't be fair to the pigs. Pigs are really very clean animals. I don't suppose you've ever kept pigs?"

"No."

She looked at the ceiling, clicking her tongue like an

angry horned owl. The room began spinning. I wondered what sort of drug she'd put in my tea. I tried my best to look her in the eye.

"Owls are from other planets," I heard myself saying.

I thought her eyes might roll out of her head and into her teacup.

Jason shut off the tape.

"Owls are from other planets?"

I shook my head.

"I don't know where that came from."

But I did know.

We had an owl for a pet once, kept it in a cage behind the house, trapped gophers and fed them to it. We liked to trap them live, Brian and I, so that we could turn them loose in the cage and watch the great bird, thing of things, essence of essences, do its bloody business—a great sweeping of wings and the claws striking, the horns pointing up like antenna.

"Owls are from other planets," Brian used to say.

I didn't tell Jason this. I didn't think it would help him to understand. In the dim light of the dashboard I saw him raise his eyebrows, then reach across and press the button to turn the tape back on.

The sparrows chattered.

"Are you crazy?"

It's a common enough question, but it is not usually asked with such gravity.

"No," I said, "I don't think so."

But then, how can one know for sure? It's difficult to be objective about these things.

"What is it about trees?" she asked.

"Pardon?"

"Do you really believe they can save the world?"

I nodded blankly, trying to decipher this. I remembered the ads I'd seen on television with Stephanie Rush as a spokeswoman for an organization that was raising funds by making noises about saving the Amazon rainforest. Her talking head looked straight into your eyes while great forests were felled mercilessly in the background.

"I'm not sure ..." I said.

"They breathe up as much air at night as they breathe out during the day. Did you ever think of that?"

"It's the filtering," I told her. "They clean the air when they breathe it in and out."

I thought her rant might lead us to the messages that Goodwin claimed Rush had sent him through his grove, and I wondered if she heard these messages too, so I wanted to keep her on the subject, but she was not impressed by my explanation.

"Maybe that's important down in that filthy city where you live now, but does it seem important here? Think of your girlhood. You came from here. Did the air seem dirty to you?"

I thought of my girlhood.

"No."

"Of course not. And trees aren't natural here anyway. This is the prairie, for goodness sakes. But you've got him planting trees all over perfectly good farm land, trying to forest the Great Plains. Now, what's the sense in that?"

"Well ..."

"And this nonsense about cattle giving off greenhouse gases. Didn't those huge herds of buffalo that were here before we got here give off greenhouse gases? I guess they were doing the right thing when they killed them all off? Is that what you've decided now? I guess you'd better make up your mind."

"You might have a point ..."

"Might? The thing you city people have to consider is that what's good for the goose isn't necessarily good for the glockenspiel. You don't understand us here. You've been away too long. But that doesn't stop you from tellin' us how to live our lives. Or telling us to give up our lives and move on. You've always been that way, you famous people, even though you can't even begin to imagine what it's like to live like us people out here in the real world."

I didn't feel real any longer. I wouldn't have been surprised if I'd flickered and disappeared altogether.

"We have to make a living, you know?" She brought her withered white hand from under the table and pointed a crooked branch of a finger at me, and the feel of that finger indicating my forehead re-established my being. "Do you understand?"

"Yes," I nodded. "You have to make a living."

"And how do you expect us to make a living by growing trees on the prairie? Answer me that!"

I couldn't. It was the mystery of the modern world she was asking me to solve, where motives no longer come down to easy equations of economics and geography; where an electric shadow can speak and people will act, even if illogically, in accord with its perceived wishes. It's something in the line of the spin that religion once put on the world: the voice from the sky that called down to a little man and told him to build a boat though he was nowhere near water—told him to kill his son though he actually kind of liked (dare I say *loved*) the little fellow.

I suppose I could have told her that. Instead, I simply shook my head. I could see her frustration building, the pupils of her eyes vibrating back and forth, trying to see two sides of me at once. What I saw in those eyes was contempt of an order I'd never before encountered.

"You don't seem to have any answers now, do you?"

"No," I said, but I could see she wanted more. "I don't know that there are any answers," I offered.

My confession only made her more angry. She stood and pointed the way to the door. "Get out of my house!"

She was right. I had nothing for her. I was an impostor. Thanking her for the tea, I got to my feet and walked in the direction she'd directed. I resisted the temptation to look back.

The fresh air steadied my head, and as I walked across the yard I blessed whatever spirit watched over me for getting me out of there alive. I really did feel saved, as though there'd been a chance she might have pushed me into the oven and turned me into rhubarb pie, but my salvation was interrupted by the sound of an engine purring, and a moment later a blue pick-up truck appeared through the trees, rolled to a stop beside me, and Goodwin stepped out.

"Hello," I said.

"Hi, Joan Swift. What're you doing here?"

He did not look pleased to see me—cocked his head sideways, owl-like, perhaps to get a different perspective.

"I was out looking at Dad's ... at our old place. I ran out of gas. Down the grid just a ways."

He scratched the corner of his mouth.

"The little Buick."

"Yeah. I was going to ask your mother …"

"Uh-huh."

"She … uh … I think she thought I was someone else."

"She's a little off."

I caught myself nodding. He spat neatly at his feet, not derisively, but perhaps to mark his territory, before he turned and walked to the shop door and picked up a small, slightly bloody stainless steel chain with two stainless steel triangles attached. He walked back toward me, the chain swaying slowly at his side. My knees felt so weak I thought I would fall.

"You'll have to wait a minute. There's a cow having trouble."

He dropped the chain in the box of the truck and motioned for me to get inside.

"You might as well come."

I nodded and got in the truck.

We followed the road allowance—two tracks overgrown with crested wheat between a pasture fenced with four strands of barbed wire and a summerfallowed field—for over a mile, spinning wildly through a couple of puddles to avoid getting stuck. The cow was laid out flat as a corpse on a dry rise not too far from the trail. He killed the engine, then sat studying the animal as she strained in dolorous futility.

"You hate to bother them but she's been at it since six this morning and I don't see nothin' showin' yet."

He took off his jacket and began rolling up his right sleeve.

Either she didn't notice his stealthy approach or she was too overwhelmed by the pain of her labour to care. He knelt behind her, lifted her tail, and reached inside her sloppy vagina with his bare arm until he was up to his elbow, rearranging things until he was able to pull out one hoof and hook on his chain. He reached in again and fished out the other hoof. Once he'd looped the chain around the second hoof, he grabbed the triangular stirrups and pulled. The cow strained along with his efforts, and when she rested he rested, and a minute later the hindquarters appeared, belly up, and a few seconds after that the head slipped out onto the ground. He picked up the calf, its white markings yellow from amniotic fluid, and hung it upside down, shaking it like a limp wet sheet to clear its lungs. At last he placed it on the ground next to the cow's head, unhooked his chains, and retreated.

"Backwards," he said through the window, "so she was pushing it right into her pelvis. But at least it was upside down. That's the way they have to come when they're backwards."

He lifted a bale from the box of the truck, threw it over the barbed wire fence, climbed through himself, carried the bale to the pair, and bedded them with dry straw. I could see on his face that he was mulling over something as he returned, but I couldn't read what it was. When he caught me watching him, he smiled.

We were halfway to the grid, just fishtailing out of the second puddle, before he spoke again. "Not a bad day to be born."

That's where the cassette runs out. It's a lovely little document, more the poetry of random noises on a March morning than something that could attest to meaning, until the statement ending it serves to lend it more profundity than any unframed moment ever had.

It sounded as though he meant himself, struggling to find his way to the light.

Or maybe he meant Joan Swift.

Apparently it didn't mean much to Jason, as he gave the cassette back to me. Later he changed his mind and asked for it, but I told him I'd thrown it away. What right did he have to it? Sure, he owned the pieces of interlocking plastic and the magnetic loop, but not the voices or the painful shrieks of cloth on vinyl when I shifted my back against the seat of Goodwin's truck. What *was* Jason's was what followed, what refused to be recorded, as if the moment were ashamed of its own vulgarity.

I'd decided I'd better start talking if I wanted to get what I wanted out of Darwin Andrew Goodwin.

"I haven't seen you in the library lately."

There was a moment's silence, an intake of breath that no one ever heard again.

"Nope," he said.

He was gripping the wheel at twelve with his right hand, his left elbow poking out the window. Loose tools and nails and spent .22 shells vibrated against the metal dash and on the floor around our feet. There was also something rattling with a particularly high pitch in the glove compartment.

"I ... uh ... you know, I didn't even recognize you that day?"

He gave me a severe sideways glance, then shrugged. "You weren't much more'n a baby when I knew you."

A jackrabbit sprang onto the trail and he swerved the truck toward it, but it deked back through the fence and escaped.

"Damn rabbits killed all my poplar saplings this winter," he said. "Cleaned the bark right off 'em. Never seen anything like it."

"I still should have recognized you. Your picture's in the paper all the time."

His lips became a thin hard line.

"I ... um ... that's part of my job. I cut stories out of the paper and put them in files. I bet you're in the paper more than anyone else around here."

Somewhat misleading: there was no Goodwin file at the library. I had never snipped his picture from a paper in my life.

"How much gas you need?" he asked.

"Oh, just a gallon. What happened with you and Stephanie Rush?"

I don't remember if he looked at me. I think not. I think he kept his eyes straight ahead, staring out the windshield; kept driving as his face slowly changed colours— became a shade of purple I'd never seen before. He drew his elbow in and strangled the wheel with both hands.

"Who sent you?"

There was a crescent wrench rattling on the dashboard that looked heavy enough to do quite a bit of damage to his skull if he reached for me.

"No one. I just ... ran out of gas."

And now he turned to face me.

"Liar," he said.

Which ought to have been enough to cure me of lying forever.

He didn't kill me, though his eyes suggested he might like to try. When we reached my father's little Buick he braked hard and everything shifted and settled.

"Get the hell out of my truck and don't you dare ever bother my mother again."

I remember being afraid that I might really be out of gas, that the claim might have made it true, but when I turned the key the engine caught. He sat there in his truck, watching me drive away.

And so, as Jason put it, I burned my *in* without getting anywhere.

"You keep it," he said, handing the cassette back to me. "It's worthless."

I shoved it into my jacket pocket.

"His mother's worthless? What he said about his calf is worthless? Couldn't that help this Hollywood guy get him right?"

He sighed.

"There's no way he's gonna talk to you again?"

"Unlikely."

"Couldn't you have been a bit subtler?"

"That's part of my beauty. I'm never subtle."

"I guess we have different aesthetics."

"Well, I hope you can find something more to your taste."

I opened the door and began to step out of the car. He grabbed my arm to stop me. We were two miles from town, parked on a side road, behind a bluff of trees where I had parked more than once with Melvin Campbell—where I had given Melvin Campbell the hickey that made him famous for a day. On this day, Jason and I hadn't even kissed, only sat there listening to the tape and discussing what had happened after the words ran out. I was being slowly crushed under the guilt of my betrayal of Mrs.

Walsh and Mrs. Goodwin and all the old ladies of the world, and now I had decided that my only chance at redemption was getting the hell out of that car.

"Let go or lose it."

I dug my nails into his hand. He yelped, released me, and, after a reflex flailing of the limb, examined his wounds.

"Jesus!" He sat there pouting, trying to massage my indentations out of his hide. "I appreciate what you did. It's just not good enough. We need to try again."

"I don't want to do it again," I said, finally reclaiming my momentum. I slammed the door and started walking toward the grid. It was a full moon, and it took only a moment for my eyes to adjust. There was a pleasantly warm breeze from the south, and I felt I could walk twenty miles. Jason pulled his car out and drove along beside me.

"Get in, Joan."

I kept marching.

"Come on. Get in the car. This is stupid. Do you wanta walk all the way to town?"

I started to run, cutting in front of him so that he couldn't get past me. He honked his horn. I retreated to the edge of the road and he pulled up beside me again.

"Get in the car, Joan."

We reached the grid and I made my turn toward town.

"Look, there's someone coming. If you're not gonna get in I'm gonna take off."

The glow of headlights bloomed on the horizon ahead.

"Go. You wouldn't want to be seen with me."

And that's what he did, accelerating away so that I had to shield my eyes from his dust. The pick-up slowed and stopped. The driver rolled down his window. Albert Munro, headed home from the bar. He knew my father, but he wouldn't likely recognize me. I could see the image of the BMW still floating in his eyes.

"You okay?"

"Fine," I said, and kept walking. He only held my receding form in his mirror for a second before he continued on his way. I wondered if he'd seen me long enough for my face to register, for it to be recorded there, on that road, on that night, in at least one other mind.

Evvy Alford married a farmer named Henry Walsh in the midst of the Depression, so it must have been true love. Or, more likely, she had got herself knocked up, like my mother, proving once again that the most important decisions in life are made between people who aren't wearing any clothes.

Henry left the farm for months at a time, doing odd jobs like trying to sell life insurance to people who never planned to die. Evvy raised the boy, Vanessa's father, through hardships that might seem incredible to us now, but were commonplace for their time. She was one of the few women who learned how to prepare the salt cod sent from Newfoundland and distributed as relief to the suffering, soaking it long enough for the salt to come out of it. She and her son were among the poorest people on earth. Of course, they didn't have to deal with an invasion of Italians, as the Ethiopians did, or a civil war, as they did in Spain, but things were bad. It never rained. Land that had once been a dream of prosperity, producing the highest quality of wheat on earth, began to turn into desert. Evvy Walsh would sweep her home three times a day to deal with the dust.

These are some of the things Susie taught me, which I learned more than a little reluctantly over the course of our last month together. I suppose I should have thanked her.

A month after my visit to Goodwin's, Susie and I finished a shift together at nine o'clock—flashed the lights to let the patrons know it was time to get out, signed out the last few books, locked the door, recorded the final figures in their proper columns, put on our jackets, punched the alarm code before we locked the door behind us, and headed home, skating along the sidewalk because the rain that day had turned to sleet and ice when the sun went down.

We had a visitor. Apparently I'd forgotten to lock the back door after I'd taken out the garbage. There was a light on in the window, and we could hear Lou Reed shouting about how rock-and-roll had saved the life of someone named Sally.

Susie wanted to call the police, but I just walked up the steps and unlocked the front door. Something in my expression must have told Susie that it was safe to join me, because she was there beside me before I could warn her away.

Jason had gathered all of the penguins and was busy lining them in formation so that two tuxedoed armies faced each other across our living-room floor. When he saw me he leaned over and muted the stereo.

"Hello, girls," he toasted us. "Just re-enacting the battle of Antarctica." He was three-quarters of the way into the bottle of Glenlivet that Brian had given me for Christmas.

Susie glared at me.

"What's this?"

I shrugged, trying my best to look innocent. I wanted to tell her that it was over, that it was already a month since the last time I'd seen him, but I couldn't very well do that. "Susie, this is Jason Warwick," I said.

He was on his feet by now, extending his hand to her.

"I used to be a reporter at the *Standard*?" That made me look: "used" to be? Susie did not seem to notice or was not interested in the qualification, and she certainly did not take his hand.

"We've met. What are you doing in my house?"

For just that one second the house was all hers: I had been evicted. She glanced down at her penguins as if she worried they might never recover from the trauma.

Jason, bless his black heart, looked crestfallen.

"Oh, I'm sorry. The back door was open. I hope you don't mind."

"Of course I *mind*. Wouldn't you mind? I should call the police."

They both looked at me, but I'd decided, rather illogically I suppose, not to become involved, and had already gone into the kitchen to put on the kettle.

"Didn't Joan tell you?" Jason said. "She and I are working on a story about Darwin Goodwin. Together. Apparently he's in love with her. She thinks he'll talk to her about Stephanie Rush."

I only had to wait a second and Susie was beside me at the stove, pinching me and hissing into my ear, "Isss that true?"

And for some reason—because I wanted to reclaim my few feet of space in *our* little house; needed to reclaim a whole part of my life that had gone missing since Evvy

Walsh had moved in (the kitchen table was still covered over with her papers, so that we'd been eating at the coffee table for weeks now)—for some reason I said, "Yeah."

"Really?"

I nodded my stubborn head.

"Well, I should get out of your way, then."

She had meant to flee back out the front door, but Jason staggered in to block her way.

"You don't have to go. I don't want to chase you out of your own home."

Instead of looking him in the eye, Susie stared into his chest, which was at her eye level. She took a deep breath.

"Murderer!" she said.

Jason gave her as innocent a look as I ever saw cross his face.

"Pardon?"

"You killed Mrs. Walsh."

Now he began to look a bit guilty, and he turned to me. I was still waiting for the kettle to boil.

"It was an accident," he said.

"Liar!"

"It was an accident. Ask Joan. She was *there*."

By the time these words were out he had already realized he should not have spoken them. Susie turned to me.

"You were there?"

"No," I said. "Of course not. I don't know what he's talking about."

Susie looked back and forth between Jason and me.

"If you were there, why didn't you tell the police?"

"No," Jason said. "Joan's right. I don't know what I was thinking. Of course she wasn't there."

He was talking to her back, as she was staring at me. I went to the cupboard and got out the teabags.

"Goodbye," Susie said.

I left the tea bags and followed her onto the step.

"You don't have to go, Susie."

"Bye," she said, darting down the stairs and bracing herself to stay upright on the icy walk. "I'll come and get my stuff tomorrow."

And she was gone, skating her way toward her parents. Within a moment her gulled form had disappeared in darkness. I called once more, "Susie!" but there was no response.

I walked back in the door to face Jason.

"Perfect," I said.

"Sorry," he said.

There was a red plastic bow attached to the neck of the Glenlivet bottle and, with all the formality of a five-star general laying a wreath on the tomb of the unknown soldier, he stuck it on my right breast.

"In honour of my liberrration," he slurred.

I looked around at my dirty laundry scattered among the penguins on the living-room floor.

"What the hell are you doing here?"

"I wanted to see you." He stepped in close and began to fumble with my buttons. I pushed him and he backed off, looking a bit sheepish. He hefted the bottle. "You making tea, or you want one of these?"

I might have kicked him out. I might have drunk my tea. I decided on Scotch.

Over drinks it gradually emerged that he'd been fired for scooping one of his own stories, a piece about the building of an inland grain terminal in Broken Head. He often made a little extra cash by selling his *Standard* stories to the *StarPhoenix*, and even though this practice was forbidden, nothing had ever happened before. He was never sure if Branchly recognized the stories and let it pass or if he was just too much of a moron to notice. This time, though, the *StarPhoenix* published the story before it appeared in the *Standard*, which is only a biweekly. "They promised it wouldn't appear till Thursday," he'd told me fifteen times before we'd finished the bottle.

Jason had become so complacent that he hadn't even bothered to rewrite the story to disguise it, so when Branchly called him into his office and laid the *StarPhoenix* beside Jason's copy for the next day's paper, there was nothing Jason could say to defend himself except, "Well, whaddaya expect, the way you bastards pay me."

"Tell you what, Warwick." Branchly smiled. "We're not gonna insult you with a paycheque any more."

"Branchly'd been looking for an excuse to get rid of me ever since I snuck through that story about closing the library. He and the mayor are such bum buddies. And I gave him the excuse he needed."

Here he was, Jason Warwick, my paramour, in my living room, on my pull-out bed, nervously eyeing the huge orange flowers printed on the cushions as if he were worried they might open their petals and swallow him, and he was trying to tell me something, but I wasn't sure what.

"So, what are you gonna do?"

He poured himself the last of the bottle.

"How'd you like to move to Toronto?" he asked.

"Me? Toronto?"

"Yeah. You."

"What about Carol?"

He glanced at the window. The curtains were closed.

"I don't think she'll want to come with us."

He smiled, and then, when I didn't return his smile, looked at the floor, at yesterday's bra wound around one leg of the coffee table where I'd dropped it, undressing as I'd watched some stupid doctor show.

"What do you say?"

I shook my head.

"You expect me to just drop my life because you come calling? You've gotta give me some time to think about this."

"That's cool. There's no panic. You're right, I do that. I react, when I should think. Let's think about it. Could I get that tape?"

I sat up straighter.

"That tape? The tape of Goodwin's mother?"

"Yeah. It's got a bit of Goodwin. They want it, anyway. They're interested in his mother. Burke says they might be able to work her in. This screenwriter guy wants to hear it, anyway."

He was still talking to my bra.

"You said you didn't want it. I threw it away."

He looked up.

"Threw it away?" I nodded. "Just … heaved it?" I nodded. "Where?"

"In the garbage."

"Recently?"

He looked toward the kitchen, hoping it might be resting there with our morning coffee grounds in a white plastic bag.

"Weeks ago."

He sighed. We sat there, silent, for five or possibly six seconds—the earth hurtling through space—before he summoned the courage and audacity to ask his next question.

"Do you want to try and do another one? Just with his mother, I mean. We'll make sure he's nowhere around. They'd pay. A lot. They were really impressed that she thought you were her."

I rose, and with all the regal magnificence I could summon, pointed toward the door.

"Get out of my house!"

I was remembering old Mrs. Goodwin directing me out of her life, trying to capture all of her electric indignity.

"Don't be melodramatic, Joan."

I was still pointing.

"There's no ..." He stopped himself, took a deep breath, and decided to try another tactic. "Listen, Joan. You're worried that your reputation has been hurt because of rumours going around about us. And maybe you've decided you want to live here. It sounds like that's what you've decided. If we do this together, that'll give us a *legitimate* reason for having been together, and it'll make people doubt the rumours. Think about it. Just like I told your friend Susie just now."

"Ohhhh ... and *she* bought it."

He rolled his eyes and motioned to her collection.

"She only buys penguins."

"Legitimate," I said, trying to load all of my scorn onto that one word.

He couldn't look at me. He stared at the floor, at the penguins marching into bloody battle, then picked up a cushion and tossed it like a basketball. The arc it made through the air had more grace than violence, but its impact erased an entire division.

"Okay. Goodbye," he said, but he didn't move.

"I loved you," I said.

I'm sure I used the past tense. I'm sure it was meant to sound like an accusation, but I doubt that's what he heard.

He slowly raised his head and looked into my eyes. Unfortunately, he did not look surprised.

"You're the most beautiful woman I've ever ... seen. I mean that. I feel so ... privileged ... just being with you. I want ... to try. We could do this story and then go. See if it works? I think you'd really like it there."

He swayed elegantly as he gave this speech, like the poplars behind our house on the farm sway when the wind blows, which it usually does. I looked at the battlefield strewn across my floor, at the T-shirt I'd worn yesterday lying in the corner. It wasn't fair that he'd come unannounced, that he'd invaded my private self that way. If I'd had some warning I could have cleaned, could have arranged things to show what I wanted him to see, to hide the parts of me that needed to be hidden. I had never felt so naked. I wanted him gone. Forever. I wanted to clobber him over the head and set that house on fire. I wanted him dead. I wanted to be dead myself. I wanted to be born again, out of that feeling he made in my gut, to be made over into a new woman without all the pitiful weaknesses of the old Joan Swift.

I shook my head.

"I'm sorry," he said before he closed the door.

And maybe he was. Maybe he really was.

I was the most beautiful woman he'd ever seen.

Can it help but be insidious, the desire to be lied to?

I have red hair, which got me teased constantly in school. Looking back it seems that most of my teenage years were spent wishing that I did not have red hair. Now it must be coming into fashion: there are redheads staring at me out of magazines all the time. Jason told me he preferred red hair, but I didn't really believe him when I saw his wife's fake platinum locks. Whose idea was that?

I do look okay, maybe even pretty, when I pose just the right way before a mirror, but all too often when someone is bold and rude enough to record my passing I am horrified by what the camera catches. And it isn't just the hair that's wrong, it's the way the head tilts, the mouth twists, the forehead wrinkles, the chin juts out as though it were pointing Scott the way to the South Pole so that he might lead in replacements for one penguin army or another. My skin is a washed-out white, blotched everywhere with obscene freckles.

Did anyone except self-indulgent philosophers worry about the problem of identity before the invention of the camera? But now everyone is the victim of its unrelenting eye, constantly smashing our illusions of who we are. It's no wonder we're all going insane.

The most beautiful woman in the world.

But no one would ever see her. And I would never see him again. Or maybe I would. Maybe I'd watch him once he moved back to the other side of the screen—watch him from some stuffy living room with a baby at my breast, and wonder what it would have been like to be inside that frame.

The next day I phoned in sick, rented one of Stephanie Rush's movies, *Blow Me Away*, and forced myself to watch. It is one of her early flicks, from when she was at the height of her career, so promising that a studio had made her the vehicle for their twenty-million-dollar gamble. I suppose the story was risqué for its day: she plays a prostitute who is won back to the straight and narrow by the love of a good man. The portrayal of the life of a working girl is warm and fuzzy in a way that only Hollywood could concoct. Or perhaps I'm wrong about that: perhaps prostitutes' lives actually are much warmer and fuzzier than most of us imagine them to be. Though I doubt it. At any rate, I didn't make it through the second hour, but it was clear what was about to happen. Too bad nothing is ever so clear in life.

I didn't succeed in finding Stephanie Rush in the film. Of course, her face and body were there, but there weren't any clues to the girl who grew up on a farm near Venus. She wasn't much of an actor, but she had the ability to hide from the camera even when she had no clothes on. There was at least something admirable in that. I wished I could be as inscrutable.

The film bombed, but the poster of her in a certain slinky yellow dress with spaghetti straps had decorated just about every teenage boy's room in America. It was not a working dress, but one she wore when she was meeting her dream man for dinner and dancing, while she was trying to hide her real identity from him. It made her look like the sexy girl-next-door boys were always peeking at over the back fence. The plot was this: she has him convinced that she works for the government. Enter one of her johns, a dark fellow with wide sideburns who sidles up to the table and

asks her to dance. Out on the floor he makes her promise
to give him a freebie or he'll tell on her. She takes him to the
washroom, stabs him with a table knife, then cuts him up
and flushes him down the toilet piece by piece.

I just made up that last part. See it yourself if you're
really interested.

So there I was watching *Blow Me Away* again the following
afternoon, the room bathed in that unearthly blue light, the
curtains all pulled to prevent the glare of the other sun
from obscuring the screen, when Susie opened the door.
She stood framed by the weatherstripping, taking me in,
my earthly remains stretched out on the bed I hadn't bothered to hide-away that morning because there seemed no
point. She also took in a few frames of Stephanie Rush
prancing across a room.

"Come for your stuff?" I asked, only to break the silence.

She nodded, her lower lip quivering slightly. She
looked around to make sure we were alone. We were. Very
much alone.

"Tell me the truth," she said. "Were you there when he
killed Mrs. Walsh?"

I did not hesitate.

"No," I said.

No saint or apostle ever made a more assured denial,
but it was not enough for Susie.

"Can you prove it to me?"

The tone of her voice suggested it was not so much a
challenge as a plea. If I could prove my innocence then she
could walk back in the door and resume her place as
though nothing had occurred. She would pass over the

invasion of Jason and any other betrayal his awful presence might have implied. It was plain enough, seeing me there, alone, so completely bereft, that he would never be back. It would be okay. As long as she was sure. As long as she knew she was eating, sleeping and residing with a woman who was innocent of Evvy Walsh's brutal murder.

"Yes," I said. "I can prove it."

I fetched the evidence from its hiding place and hit the stop button on *Blow Me Away*, which is as far into it as I ever reached, and I pushed in the new tape and hit the play button. Susie sat down on the edge of my bed to watch.

The door flies open and there I am in the bathtub, my face registering shock and anger, and I'm shouting abuse, curling my arms around my flesh to hide myself, turn myself into a large pink amoeba, and I plead, humiliated, but without humility, and I'm almost weeping through my rage at the moment I stand and display my bare naked body for the camera and then lunge at the cameraman and fall, lie there, not moving, breathing my last breath, the sneaker nudging my head failing to rouse me, before the panicked retreat out the door.

"You see," I said to Susie, whose expression revealed that she did not see. "I couldn't have been there. I've been dead for years."

Susie rose slowly to her feet, the way the living rise on first realizing they are in the presence of the dead. She went into the kitchen and gathered Evvy Walsh's papers off the table, stuffing them all into a cardboard box that she paused with, hugging it against her chest, as she stood at the door.

"I'm going now," was all she said.

And she went away without taking her own things.

My mother's condominium is in the new subdivision on the south side, nestled in a ridge at the edge of the creek valley. The building, a series of rowhouses with redundant sloping roofs, was supposed to look like a chalet, and the developers had named the complex Alpine Village. When I showed up at her door that evening my mother was so surprised and happy to see me that she ushered me straight into the bedroom to show me the enlargement she'd just had framed and hung over her dresser. It was a dog, a wet Irish setter with mournful eyes, standing between the rails on some remote branch line.

"What do you think?"

"It's … beautiful."

"Do you really think so?"

"Yes. I like his eyes."

"It's Dr. Doidge's dog. Evan. Why would they name a dog Evan?" she asked and then immediately answered herself: "I imagine it has something to do with the fact that they've never had children, but I've never pried too deeply into that little mystery. I took him for a walk out near the farm so that I could get some pictures of the branch line before they tear it up. Did you know they were tearing it up?"

"No."

"You really like it?"

"Yes."

"I think it's pretty good. I think it's one of the better things I've done."

She led me into the living room where she offered me a place to sit and a drink.

"Can I get you a drink?" she said to me, her daughter.

"Tea would be nice," I replied, perched stiffly on the edge of her sofa.

"Tea?" she said. "Yes, tea would be lovely, wouldn't it?"

She swooped off to the kitchen.

When the tea was ready, waiting on her silver tray in her silver service with an array of cookies and squares spread out to complement, she sat down across from me with her steaming cup and said, "So ... what brings Joan out for a visit on such a ... dark night?"

I chose a fig newton, then abandoned it for a date square.

"I was wondering ... if you could do me a favour?"

She slid forward on her chair, eager, expectant.

"A favour. Certainly. Yes. Of course. What is it?"

"Could you help me make a dress?"

She glowed.

"A dress! Of course. What sort of dress? Do you have a pattern?"

"I'll show you," I said, zipping open my bag to take out the videotape. She watched silently, a little bemused, as I pushed it into her machine and punched the required buttons, cutting the volume completely. I'd already cued the movie to the proper spot.

"Could you make me a dress *exactly* like that one?"

The yellow fabric swirled around Stephanie Rush's hips as her dream man turned her about the dance floor. My mother didn't reply until they were seated again, sipping their cocktails.

"What's this about?"

"I need a dress like that one."

"That's Stephanie Rush."

"Yes."

"I don't like the sound of this. What's going on, Joan? Are you still involved with Jason Warwick? I thought you told me it was all over."

"I need that dress," was all I could say. "Will you help me?"

There was a gas fireplace in Mother's condominium, which still contained the same romantic log I'd burned a hundred times the year I'd lived there, and there were pictures of Brian and me ranged across the mantelpiece. She walked to one of these now, a photo of me at fourteen, holding up a pike I'd caught in the creek, and she gazed into that fish's eyes.

"What did I do? What did I do to make you so stupid? Was it because I never drilled you with flash cards like some of the other mothers did for their girls? Was that it? Or was it the unstimulating environment I was forced to bring you up in?"

It looked as though she'd rehearsed this a thousand times. I pressed the eject button on her remote.

"Forget it."

Yanking the tape from the machine, I made a show of getting ready to go. She was still standing there at her fireplace, watching me stuff the video back into my bag.

"Do you really love him?"

"What difference does it make?"

"You're gonna get hurt, Joan. You're gonna get hurt very badly."

I shrugged.

"Isn't that what love's all about?"

She sighed.

"I have no idea what love's all about. Why don't you tell me?"

"Forget it."

"No, I mean it. Please, tell me. I promise I won't say a word until you've had your say."

And so I told her Jason's story, about how he'd tracked me down when he heard that Darwin Goodwin was in love with me, and he'd come to me with a plan to get Goodwin's mother to talk so that we could unearth the untold story. Together. I told her the story that legitimated us.

And she wanted so badly to believe it that she did.

"So you haven't been having an affair?"

"No. Never. We've just been planning this, and I even managed to get a tape of Goodwin, but I never managed to get him to tell us anything, so now we're gonna try again. With this dress. If you'll help me." She looked at me, her mouth open in an expression of awful gullible wonder.

"I think maybe I am falling in love with him," I said.

"Oh, Joan, you silly fool," she said, and she wrapped her arms around me the way she'd done when I was eight and I'd fallen off my bike and skinned my elbow, "It does not pay to fall in love with a married man."

This statement emerged with such weary wisdom that I had to wonder where it came from—what dark corner of experience in this woman I called my mother.

"You make it sound as though you know this personally," I said into her shoulder.

"Personally?" she repeated the word. "Yes. My good doctor has taught me so much."

As she made her confession she gripped me even harder. The pasty man with the brown eyes that were always looking through you. How had I not seen it?

What could she possibly see in him?

"Is *he* why you left Dad?"

I pushed away to look at her, but her face had already fixed itself into her stern motherly pose.

"I've told you, Joan. Your father and I felt it was time to pursue our own lives."

"But did the life you were pursuing involve Dr. Doidge?"

She backed away from me and took a deep breath.

"Your father and I don't love each other any more."

"That's not true. He loves you."

She cleared her throat.

"Do you still want me to help you with this dress?"

And so for the next two days I was the daughter she'd always wanted, tracing patterns and cutting cloth and matching diamonds and stabbing myself with pins and needles.

I had to go to Regina to buy the wig. They're not cheap. I showed the clerk the photo of Stephanie Rush.

"Oh, retro!" she said.

"Yeah," I said. "Retro."

"Cool."

I called Jason at home.

"Who is this?"

"You know who it is."

"You're not to call me here. Ever."

"I am calling you there. Now."

"What is it?"

"Can I come over?"

"No!"

"Can you come over here, then?"

"No! Of course not."

"Why not?"

"Leave it alone, Joan. Why beat a dead horse?"

"For the joy of the sound of the whip on his hide."

He hung up. I dialled the number again. I had it memorized.

"Hello."

It was a tense but careful hello: a hello that was only ninety-nine per cent sure of who it was being directed toward and was taking care of the one per cent.

"I'll do it," I said.

The silence held long enough that I wondered if he would hang up again without responding.

"You'll do what?"

"I'll be your Stephanie Rush. And then we'll go away together. But you have to come over. Now."

An hour later I watched him shuffling up my walk in his black trenchcoat, collar high, his shoulders hunched against the peering suspicious eyes of all my peering suspicious dead neighbours. I wish I had a picture of his face when I opened the door. They could have used it on the back cover of his book.

"Is that *you*?"

"Does it look okay?"

He didn't answer at first, just slowly nodded with a dazed expression on his face.

"Blond hair suits you."

"I thought you liked red hair."

"I do. But blond hair looks … great on you."

"Do I look like Carol?"

He ignored that, stood back to make a serious appraisal, his hand on his chin.

"You look like *her*. You look better than her. You look like her twenty years ago."

I smiled. She smiled.

"Do you want me to leave the wig on?" I asked him after he'd removed the dress, his mouth moving across my navel. He paused to look up at me.

"Well. You don't ... have to."

I licked a finger and, as though turning a page, touched the tip of his nose.

"Do you want me to?"

He shook his head.

"If ... you want to."

And so he made it *my* act, *my* decision—my responsibility. He was only a willing disciple in what happened there on Susie's queen-sized mattress. And something did happen. There was all that had come before, but now there was also all that had yet to come, mingled together into one transmogrifying present: the intimate use of the five senses to their most exquisite rendering in all the range of human experience. You might expect that there would be less intimacy because I was wearing that wig, that he was thinking of her when he should have been thinking of me, but that's not right at all. I was still me and he was still with me, but I had also literally become the fantasy of her that all of those boys had hung on their bedroom walls—the fantasy that all of those men, and women too, wanted, but had never been able to reach, until he touched me. And as I stared down into his eyes and said those three words, "I love you," I said them not only for him, but for all of the millions who had ever sought after my love only to find paper or the cold impregnability of a screen, and I became for that moment the physical manifestation of love that could heal all of the wounded hearts of the world.

And he whispered back, "Me too."

And he did. At least for that instant, he did.

Afterwards we were both too ashamed and embarrassed to face one another.

Jason immediately began getting dressed.

"I don't know," he said in response to nothing. "Maybe you should do it tomorrow. He has to be in court so you can be sure he won't be at the farm. It couldn't be safer."

Goodwin had a court appearance the next morning for violating his restraining order. Apparently he'd called the number of Stephanie Rush's agency 176 times in a one-week period.

"Okay," I said. "Tomorrow."

"Or don't you feel ready? I don't want to rush you. Whenever you feel ready. If tomorrow's not good there'll be other times."

He sniffed his armpit, then picked up Susie's deodorant from her dresser.

"That's not mine."

He looked at me to see if I was serious. He set the deodorant back down.

"Sorry."

I didn't excuse him. Hurriedly, he buttoned up his shirt.

"Well, whatever you think."

"I'm ready," I said. "Tomorrow'll be fine. Have you already told Carol?"

"Told her ...?"

"That you're leaving."

"No," he said, and when he saw my eyes he turned away. "It's not that easy. We've been together a long time. I gotta run. I'll call *you*."

He stepped out the door, leaving me lying there in the rumpled pink quilt Susie's mother'd made for her, my blond scalp hanging on her bedpost.

The Broken Head Courthouse presides over the lower regions of the north slope of the creek valley, a rather pretentious neoclassical affair, with a magnitudinous granite staircase no doubt meant to warn the approaching penitent of the relentless approach of God's kingdom—of His stone steps—and to remind her that there might not be a welcome mat waiting when the time came for her to knock on His grand doors.

I had only been there twice before: once on a tour with the Girl Guides, and once when I was subpoenaed for the trial of a classmate who had murdered his girlfriend when she threatened to break up with him. In the end I wasn't actually called, as someone else's testimony made my measly contribution redundant.

That day, I was late. I'd kept staring at myself—at my ridiculous imitation of her—in the mirror, wondering what it was they all wanted from her, or from me, and where they had lost whatever it was that they needed to find in us. By the time I'd left the house, the hearing had already started. When I stepped from my father's car, a businessman walking past did a double take. He kept walking, glancing back every now and then as I balanced myself across the street in those absurdly high heels.

A murmur rumbled around the courtroom as I pushed open the door and stepped inside. One by one, people began turning around and staring at me. Goodwin turned, then Jason, and as Jason's eyes met mine his face became the same bleached shade that I imagined his skull would one day be. Finally, everyone in the room was looking at me. I looked at my feet. I think I may have blushed. The judge beat his gavel on his desk and called for order. When things quieted down the judge spoke directly to me.

"Madam, you'll have to leave. I will not have my courtroom turned into a circus."

I know. It sounds like something a judge would say in one of those stupid courtroom dramas, but he actually said it. You can't blame him, really. He'd obviously learned as much from Hollywood about being a judge as the rest of us have learned from Hollywood about being ourselves. At any rate, by that time all I wanted to do was leave, and when I did, Jason and the other twenty-three reporters followed me.

"Miss? Missss? Why are you dressed that way? Why are you dressed like Stephanie Rush?"

They mobbed me, jostled me, tried to block my way, once even knocked me down so that I had to grab my wig to hold it on, then slip off my shoes and rise again, carrying them, while all the time they thrust their mikes in my face, shouting their questions. All those sweaty reporters from Regina, Saskatoon, Edmonton, Calgary, Winnipeg, Toronto, New York and Los Angeles. The chamber of commerce should have given Goodwin some sort of honorary membership for all the business he was bringing to town.

I said nothing. Not that it mattered. The television guys filmed me, the print guys photographed me, and the radio guys recorded my presence in their own words, speculating on my significance to the state of humanity.

I had never had so much significance.

Jason stood back against a limestone wall, taking notes.

When I had finally run the gauntlet, back down those endless steps, I got into the car and drove away. The reporters recorded it all in case it might be useful.

I went home, undressed, and dressed again, then went to the library for the afternoon. I'd originally called in sick, but now I told Wanda I was beginning to feel better and had decided it was time to get back to work.

"Bad flu," she said.

"Yeah, I couldn't hold a thing down."

She nodded.

"Susie's still not better. I guess her parents are looking after her."

I nodded. She was looking at me in a way that made me very uncomfortable.

"Did you get your hair cut?" she asked.

"No."

"Oh. You look ... different," she said.

I nodded.

"I am."

She retreated to her information desk.

As it turned out, that was my last day of work.

When I got home, I watched myself on the six o'clock news. Mom was the first to call.

"I saw you on the news, dear."

"Oh ..."

"Well ... the dress looked lovely."

"Thank you."

"Is this ...? Aren't you afraid that people might recognize you? Aren't you afraid of what people might think?"

"What might people think?"

"That dressing up like Stephanie Rush is ... unusual behaviour. I thought you said you were going to talk to his mother?"

"We changed the plan. People won't recognize me."

"You're not going to talk to *him?* Not alone. He's dangerous, Joan."

"No. I'm still talking to his mother, but we needed to do this first."

"Joan. I don't like the sounds of this. ..."

"Listen, I've gotta go, Mom."

"I don't like this one little bit. I hope you know what you're doing, dear, because ..."

I hung up. The phone immediately rang again.

"So what was that all about?" Jason.

"What did it look like?"

"A spectacle. A ridiculous performance for the cameras."

"How can you be Stephanie Rush without a camera to help?"

"Jesus, Joan! What good did that do? The plan was to get a tape of his mother. Now he'll be watching for you."

"Now everyone will be watching for me. Now I'm legitimate."

And I hung up on him.

The news inside the courtroom that day was that Goodwin, who no longer trusted lawyers and was acting as his own legal counsel, had asked for a delay in the proceedings until he'd completed his seeding, basing his request on his concern for the economic welfare of his elderly mother, and Judge Richardson granted this delay with the proviso that Goodwin would not attempt to contact Ms. Rush again.

Goodwin had not seeded all his earth to trees. His is good land, better than any my father ever owned. It was impossible not to think of my father—of the picnics of sandwiches and fruit and oatmeal cookies and thermoses of hot strong tea we'd taken to him in the field—as I drove toward Goodwin's antique cabless tractor. His fourteen feet of cultivator swirled up grey clouds of dust into the evening sky. At the four corners of his field, where the tractor turned, Goodwin had left a series of uncultivated triangles of baked weedy soil. I drove onto the field from the northwest corner, following a progression of these weedy triangles, knowing that he'd have to work over them when the field was finished and he'd erase my tire tracks when he did. This was a trick I'd learned from my father. Don't misunderstand: the trick wasn't designed to conceal a passing, but to save the soil from unnecessary pulverization. This is the prairie. Give the earth an excuse to blow away and it will.

I parked the car on the packed and weathered soil in the centre of the field, infested here and there with patches of pigweed, mustard, buckwheat and Russian thistle, and I waited for him to come around again. When he was within a quarter mile I got out of the car and stood there. Posing. I'd been imagining this part, from his point of view, for days now. After all these years of waiting and wanting and needing and chasing and expectation and anticipation and frustration and rejection—and for how many of us does rejection mean a literal jail?—now here I was, standing in his field. The wind caught the yellow dress and swirled it up like dust lifting into the blue. I tiptoed over the land he'd already worked, my yellow spike heels sinking straight into the topsoil, then knelt and lifted a lump of that black soil and crumbled it between my fingers, squeezed it into a lovely black lump the way I'd seen my father do. Then the tractor reached me and the dust caught me and I had to close my eyes. When I opened them again Goodwin had climbed down and taken the few steps to me and he stood there, gazing for a moment, before he grabbed my arm and dragged me toward the car. His lips moved, but I couldn't hear him over the roar of the tractor.

"Get your hands off me!" I screamed and he must have heard despite the noise, because he released me, then leaned close, as if he were about to kiss me, and shouted these words in my ear:

"Who do you think you are?"

"Me!" I shouted back.

He seemed to consider this for a moment, then continued on to the car and got in the passenger side. I followed him and got behind the wheel. He had opened my glove compartment and was shuffling through the contents.

"What do you want?" he said.

"Nothing. I just want to talk."

"Who sent you?"

"No one."

He found the registration.

"Stanley Swift," he read out loud.

He turned and eyed me with surprise, and it was plain he really hadn't recognized either me or the car. His eyes narrowed.

"What would your daddy say?"

I shook my head.

"Don't bring my father into it."

He threw the registration back and brought out a pen with the name of an insurance company written on it, examining that as though it might be another clue. "Did you think I was stupid enough to think you were her?"

"I am her," I said. "I'm as much her as she is."

This gave him pause.

"What do you mean by that?"

"I mean that the woman you're after never existed. You just made her up inside your head."

His face began moving in a thousand directions at once and then he started jabbing his finger, trying to punch a hole in my aura.

"You dress up like Stephanie and come traipsing out into my field, and you've got the nerve to tell me that *I'm* crazy? Well, I'm gonna call the police about this little episode and if you come near this place again you'll find yourself locked up in a tidy little cell. How would you like that?"

I smiled serenely.

"You mean, you're going to do to me what she's done to you?"

He pursed his lips, nodding at something I'd apparently confirmed for him—a depth of depravity he'd only suspected before, but now knew to exist.

"You don't know nothing about it."

"I'd like to."

"I'll bet you would."

He was staring at the spot where the hem of my dress rested against my upper leg. I pulled it straight.

"I'm not saying you're crazy. I'm just saying that she's only a fantasy. You've never really known her. She's just ... an image of a woman."

He glanced at my face, then looked nervously away.

"I don't need your amateur psychology. I've heard it all before. I know her better than I know anyone else on the face of the earth. Except maybe myself."

The tractor began gasping for fuel, revving three ferocious roars before it gave up and died. He'd turned off the gas line. You've got to let a tractor cool off slowly or you'll warp your engine block.

In the absence of all that sound I could hear my heart beating in my ears.

"So, are you saying that you actually met Stephanie Rush?"

"Course I met her."

"Met her like you're meeting me right now? She was this close?"

He glanced at me again, then looked straight ahead. He might have been trying to make out the number on the tag of one of his cows standing next to the fence at the edge of the field.

"Closer."

He was not even breathing.

"Then why does she deny it?"

He took the pen out of the glove box again, scribbled on his palm, studied the blue ink, then put the pen back again.

"Her husband. Because of her husband."

"So, why do you refuse to tell the story?"

"Because I promised her I wouldn't."

Of course, his eyes said. How could you be so stupid?

"But she betrayed you. She's never defended you."

He smiled derisively, watching the horizon, not me.

"You wouldn't understand."

"No, I don't."

And he looked me in the eye.

"I love her. Don't you understand *love*, Joan Swift?"

I had to look away.

"Then why do you keep bothering her?"

"You can only hide from the truth for so long before it hunts you down."

"And you're the truth?"

"In her case, I am."

I had turned west just in time to see the sun kiss the horizon, gilding the broken cloud. I knew he wanted to tell me and that he would tell me and that all I had to do was ask.

"I believe you. And I also believe that I'm your truth. You promised her that you'd never tell anyone her story. But I'm here, and I really believe that I really am as much her as she ever was, so what's stopping you from telling our story to me?"

It was as thin a tissue of logic as has ever been unfurled, but what made it so convincing was that I knew it was true.

"You're crazy," he said.

I shrugged.

"Takes one to know one."

He frowned, and slowly, with all the gravity of the world's wisest and most basely abused man, shook his tired head.

And then he told me.

D espite Stephanie's determination to push on with these ambitious new projects, 1975 would be a year of unending problems, beginning with her struggles with the studio for her fair share of the profits arising from the unexpected success of Pop Goes the Weasel, and extending to what, at the time, seemed a trivial matter of an annoying Canadian fan who climbed the wall of their estate and was attacked and slightly mauled by the guard dogs.

But Darwin Andrew Goodwin was to become a nightmare Stephanie would never awaken from. At first, his deranged insistence that she did—must—love him seemed a mere inconvenience: after all, she had all the power that money and fame can buy, and Goodwin must have represented only a quaint reminder of the world she had escaped so many years before. Her quote of that summer to The Los Angeles Times that Goodwin "seems like a nice man, but I have no idea where he thinks he met me" attests to how insignificant she originally *thought him to be. But he, like her past, would not release her.*

As we have already seen, Russel Burlitz was prone to fits of jealousy. Maurice Folger, Stephanie's longtime bodyguard, reported that Burlitz warned her almost daily that if she were ever unfaithful to him there would be no second chance: "I am not a man to be made a fool of." So when a farmer from Saskatchewan turned up, claiming that he was having a relationship with Stephanie, despite all the evidence to the contrary, Burlitz's suspicions were aroused, and their marriage was immediately put under severe stress.

Burlitz's first thought was revenge, and he began an affair with Barbara Mann, the star of Noble Forgotten, *which he was directing, on location in Mexico, at the time. It was the beginning of a series of affairs he would have with other actresses that stretched over the course of the remainder of Stephanie's life, right up until the day she died.*

Stephanie read accounts of his tryst with his leading lady in the tabloids, along with gossip about her own supposed affair with Goodwin. Her agent, Bartley Morrison, recalls that she did not take any time off, as he advised her to do, but continued trying to find backers for Lonely Moon. *Faced with Burlitz's betrayal and his lack of faith, she met the press's ongoing allegations with stoic pride, stubbornly fighting for her marriage, insisting that she had never met the man, and that whatever relationship he imagined they were having was merely a delusion. Regrettably, Burlitz was not so easily persuaded, and*

Goodwin's refusal to reveal the details of their affair only made her task more difficult: specifics would have been easy to refute, whereas his cryptic statements made everything seem possible.

An excerpt from
Make Believe Love
by Jason Warwick

[Thursday, June 15th]

Darwin Andrew Goodwin, finally resigned
to the impossibility of anything so beautiful
as love surviving on this planet, is ready to go home, ready
to turn his back on the city of dark angels forever, when
someone knocks on his motel room door. He's contemplat-
ing the exact moment of his departure while he stretches
out on the lumpy mattress, watching the women's roller
derby between the dirty white toes of his grey woollen work
socks, when the proverbial knock of opportunity takes him
by surprise. Feeling a bit bloated from too much of what
Americans choose to call beer, he stumbles to the door,
opens it, and peers out into the night.

It's Stephanie Rush.

Who is she, this real Stephanie Rush, standing there
silhouetted by blue neon? How does she differ from the
woman he has watched projected on screens, the woman who
comes to him in waves to be reintegrated by his television

set, and the flesh-and-blood woman who will one day
come to meet him in his field? What separates this unex-
purgated, unedited Stephanie from all her other selves? Is
it the way she massages her temples with her fingertips—
the silver nail polish moving in tiny perfect circles—when
he sits her on the bed and urges her to breathe deeply and
calmly, and sound out slowly what she is trying to tell him?

"You might offer me a drink," she finally says.

He looks sheepishly at the wastebasket full of empty
beer cans, then fetches her some water from the bathroom,
tearing the paper wrapper from the last clean glass.

"It's all I've got," he explains as he offers the virgin high-
ball. She sniffs it suspiciously.

"Not like the water back home on the farm," she says.

"You had good water?"

"Terrible. Iron bacteria. Tasted like there'd been rusty
nails soaking in it."

Her throat does an exquisite dance as she drinks down
the whole glass, then gasps for air.

"You have to get me out of here. He'll find us. He has
eyes … everywhere."

"In the back of his head …" Darwin offers.

She thinks about this.

"No," she says. "Not there."

He bundles his clothes and bundles Stephanie into his
pick-up (perhaps illogical in a hot California night, but
something about the act of concealment demands this
bundling) and they speed through a maze of intersections to
elude their pursuers, with Stephanie calling out directions—
"Turn here. Turn here!"—but all to no avail, because his
ridiculously out-of-place twenty-year-old half-ton, with the

ridiculously out-of-place licence plate, is already trapped in their headlights. It's not the truck for a chase, as it tops out at fifty-five, so the director's hired guns have no problem keeping up and, when they tire of the pursuit, trying to force him off the road. It's Stephanie who solves this problem: she rolls down the window and, with a tiny .22 calibre pistol she takes from her purse, fires a lead projectile that explodes their windshield into an opaque web of blue interstices.

They don't follow any more.

The desert greets them with a full moon bright enough to reveal them to anyone within a thousand miles, except there is no one to see, for they have reached the end of the world and might fly off any minute to be swallowed up by the sky and become a constellation that lovers would be willing to gamble their lives on.

Which is when they run out of gas.

He had no time to think about buying fuel, and the last-chance station was long since chanced. They stumble from the truck and strike out across the desert. Hours later, Stephanie is overcome by exhaustion and he allows her to stop and catch some sleep on the sand. The desert nights are cold. Darwin builds a fire from scraps of mesquite. He slaps himself across the face, trying to stay awake, but before long he nods off.

A yipping awakes him. They are surrounded by a pack of wild dogs, teeth bared between black lips, ribs jutting like the waves on the dunes. He slowly reaches for Stephanie's purse, pulls out her make-up kit, her little black book, her birth control pills, her vibrator, her amphetamines, her calculating machine, a pacifier, a live garter snake, a dog-eared copy of Sartre's *Being and Nothingness*, before he finally finds the pistol. He aims it into the sky and pulls the trigger. It's empty. Instinctively, he grabs a branch of mesquite and attacks the lead dog. The other dogs crouch back on their haunches, waiting for a victor. Meanwhile, Stephanie sleeps on, blissfully unaware. The fight is a long one, with Darwin getting the worst of it, but in the end, as they grapple in a death embrace, he brings out his trusty jackknife—no self-respecting farmer would be caught dead without his jackknife in his pocket—and stabs the beast to death. It jerks its last spasms of life in his bloody arms. The other dogs turn tail and run.

By this time Stephanie has woken and she rushes to him. He lies with his head in her lap while she nurses his many wounds. Moaning her name a thousand times over, he finally blacks out from the unbearable pain.

The blistering heat of the desert sun beats down on him when he awakens again. Stephanie has bandaged his wounds with strips of her Halston original and poulticed them with an unguent concocted from a cactus she discovered by digging in the sand. They have no water, unhappily, and Darwin is sure they should head for the highway, but Stephanie insists she's heard of a secret settlement not far north of here. Besides, her husband's men will be waiting for them at the highway. They head north, the vultures circling overhead.

Sand.

More sand.

Still more sand.

Their footprints stretch behind them all the way to their birth. Before them, the horizon ripples in the distance, but nothing ever gets closer. Just when it seems they will surely die they see something poke into view: the settlement! Darwin, overcome by his wounds, crumples to the sand.

"Save yourself," he mumbles before the black void overcomes him.

A stream of water is being directed into his mouth when he awakens. A crowd of men stand around in fatigues while Stephanie revives him with cool water from a clay vessel.

They are saved!

However, as he becomes stronger an overheard conversation reveals to him that the settlement is actually the headquarters of a secret anarchist organization intent on overthrowing the U.S. government, and that they plan to star Stephanie in a propaganda campaign. Stephanie refuses to be so used and they lock her and Darwin in a dungeon dug under the main compound. Darwin will not be stopped—not without a fight—and he digs his way to safety with the help of a badger he befriended while they were in the desert (yes, this should have been mentioned earlier, but it must have happened somewhere during their trek northward over all that sand) and then he foils the plan by single-handedly killing six men and snapping the spines of three more on the way to breaking into the radio room and signalling the FBI. At which point, the anarchist leader enters, a huge man with a bullfrog tattooed on his forehead, and Darwin and he engage in a gargantuan battle during which Darwin is nearly killed before the leader trips and falls backwards, impaling his bullfrog on a steel reinforcing rod.

Unfortunately, this entire eventuality also foils Darwin's own plans of living happily ever after with Stephanie, as the FBI spirit her away to her husband and tell Darwin to go home to Canada and forget the whole unfortunate incident—it seems that the anarchists were actually FBI agents intent on overthrowing their own government and what Darwin and Stephanie have stumbled upon is bigger than both of them—big enough to crush any tiny love affair. Darwin knows too much. He's lucky they don't just finish him off. But the anarchists let him live, because even if he tells his story, nobody will believe it: everybody will think he's crazy.

So, there you go. That's exactly what happened. Or, at least, that's what Darwin Andrew Goodwin told me that day in Dad's car. All except the part about the badger. I added that because I thought the tale needed an animal friend. To balance off the mad dogs, you know? And to placate the SPCA and the animal rights lobby.

You don't believe me?

You refuse to suspend your disbelief?

Sorry. I thought maybe that's what you wanted. I guess I had you confused with that mob who take such pleasure in watching some star act out some writer/producer/director's megalomaniacal wish-fulfilment fantasies. Why don't they lock up those guys?

I do apologize. I guess Mother's impending visit is sharpening my edge. She's coming for supper tonight.

Sarcasm, Mom always tells me, is the lowest form of humour.

Sorry. Here's what really happened:

As Goodwin wanders the streets, drunk on that watery elixir of some polluted artesian well, who should he spot through the window of one of those exclusive restaurants on Sunset Boulevard but the real living Stephanie Rush having dinner with her director husband. Darwin stands for a moment, watching her through the glass, not quite believing his eyes. Yes, it's her. The way she sweeps her hair back from her eyes is unmistakable. It really is her. Mesmerized, he gazes wistfully through the glass until he feels a sudden craving for popcorn.

He bursts into the restaurant, past the alarmed maître d', and marches straight to her table.

"I'm the friend of your parents who wanted to visit you and I need to know why you didn't even have the decency to return my calls."

Stephanie, about to bite into some sort of bird's nest, pauses.

"Pardon?"

"I'm a friend of your Mom and Dad's ..."

At which point he is interrupted by a bodyguard wrapping an arm around his throat.

"Just a second ..." Stephanie is on her feet. "Let go of that man."

Reluctantly, the bodyguard obeys. Darwin attempts to straighten his collar.

"Do you really know Mom and Dad?"

"Yeah. I helped your dad fix his tractor last month."

"Really? Which one?"

"The Case front-end loader."

"Is he still using that thing? It should have been melted down years ago and made into jewellery for professional ball players. Are you from Venus?"

"No, Broken Head."

"Really? Broken Head." She turns to her husband.

"We got caught in a blizzard there once on our way to my aunt's for Christmas."

Her famous neurotic husband doesn't deign to look up from his frog's legs.

"My, isn't that fascinating. Small world."

Stephanie turns back to Darwin and adjusts his collar to something approximating its natural state.

"We were holed up in the Ukrainian Orthodox church for two nights until it blew over. I couldn't believe they had a Ukrainian Orthodox church in Broken Head. It even had the onions on the roof."

"They have more churches per capita in Broken Head than any other city in North America," Darwin says, feeling her cool fingers brushing his neck. Someone once told him this about the churches. He has no idea if it is actually true. Stephanie, happily, is suitably impressed.

"Really? Well, it is the Bible belt."

The bodyguard stands ready, apparently waiting for the pleasantries to end so that he can complete his task by dragging Darwin away and pummelling him soundly before tossing him in the alley for the rats to nibble.

"Well, sit down, sit down," Stephanie insists.

Her husband looks up, alarmed.

"Stephanie! If you don't mind, I'd like some privacy."

"That's fine, dear." She turns to the bodyguard. "Could you find my husband a table where he can have some privacy.?"

She pulls out a chair for Darwin and motions for him to sit. Her husband releases an affected sigh.

"I don't think we got your name, Mr.—?" Stephanie says.

Darwin tells her his name and they launch into a glorious conversation about the weather on the Prairies and the price of wheat and the plague that decimated the gopher population last year and the health of Stephanie's parents. The bodyguard skulks away to a safer distance and the waiter gives Darwin a menu. It's in a foreign language, so he simply orders a cup of coffee. Stephanie's husband eats sullenly, never offering a word. Finally, he calls the waiter and asks for the bill.

"But I'm not ready to go," Stephanie tells him. "Darwin and I are still chatting."

He sighs the mother of all sighs.

"You know I have a very busy day tomorrow, Steph."

"But I don't."

And yet another sigh.

"Well, at any rate, I have to get home. If you want to stay longer, I'll have Miles come back for you after he drops me off."

"Don't bother. I'll catch a cab."

"I can drop ya," Darwin volunteers.

"Darwin'll drop me. Don't worry about it. And take Brutus with you." She points to the bodyguard.

Her husband glares for a three count before he responds.

"Fine. I'll see you later."

He gets up, confers with the bodyguard and escorts him away, leaving Stephanie to finish her dessert and converse further on the hidden meaning of *Pop Goes the Weasel*—perhaps her most popular film. The writer, a devoted Catholic, had the Virgin Mary in mind when he created Stephanie's character. The chase scene that begins in the disco was meant to represent the flight into Egypt. Darwin, of course, finds this all very fascinating.

When they're finished she pays the bill and Darwin escorts her out to his Fargo. Darwin wishes he'd cleaned the bailer twine out of the back before he left Saskatchewan, but Stephanie quickly calms his anxiety with a slap on the fender.

"Nice machine. They don't make 'em like this any more."

They get in and he starts toward her place, but she tells him no, she doesn't want to go home just yet, but instead would like to take him to this special place she knows. She directs him through the maze of turnpikes and up the side of the San Gabriels, until they're in the sky, looking down at the sun setting into the thick bank of yellow smog blanketing the city.

"Beautiful," Darwin says.

"Yeah," Stephanie agrees. "I want to live up here, looking down on all that filth."

Darwin nods as he gazes out over that glorious vista of golden light.

"This must be what it's like in Heaven."

All at once she begins to weep. He takes her in his arms and she sobs all her terrible grief into his shoulder. Finally she gets control of herself, dabbing at her eyes, embarrassed.

"I'm sorry. I hate it here so much."

"But then why don't you escape it altogether? Why don't you come back to the Prairies?"

"I want to. I really do. This is his town. It's never been mine. I'm just a prisoner here. But … he'd never leave it. So, I thought, at least I can get this far away from it. At least I can…."

He stops her words with a kiss.

They make love in the chaparral.

Afterwards, she wants to flee immediately, to return to his farm in Broken Head where she will live happily ever after in a baby-blue bungalow, baking pies and making babies. It's Darwin who insists that she go back and tell her husband that it's over. He wants to do the right thing and he thinks this is the right thing to do. At last she agrees. He drives her home and she tells him she'll meet him at his motel the next morning.

The next morning she doesn't show. Frantic, he drives back to the estate and buzzes the security, but when he gives his name they tell him they have no appointment registered for him and he will not be admitted. He doesn't know what to do. He climbs over the wall and makes his way toward the mansion. That's when the dogs get him. He tries to beat them off with a palm frond, but he's maimed in the process and would be torn to pieces if it weren't for the intervention of his trusted badger Edward G., who has followed him all the way from Saskatchewan, catching rides and eating small children and having many lovely adventures along the way—but that's another tale.

The next day he tells the police his story. Someone in the LAPD must be an informant for *The National Enquirer* because next thing he knows a reporter from that esteemed publication is by his bed taking pictures and asking questions. When they interview Stephanie Rush, she denies ever having met him in her life.

Everybody—even *The National Enquirer*—concludes that he is crazy.

You're getting annoyed.

I'm sorry, but I find that I can't tell you. He promised Stephanie Rush that he would keep the story secret. He didn't mean for you to know, so how can I justify selling it to you? Even to pay for his freedom.

What would you think of me if I were to break that promise?

Sometimes, maybe, we have no right to the truth.

What made me want to write this book was the empathy I gained for Stephanie's plight after being subjected to exactly the same sort of delusional fantasy of love. In telling her story, I was telling my own.

How, I have been asked, could there be two erotomaniacs in that one small Prairie town?

I cannot say. It must be something in the water. That would certainly explain the smell.

An excerpt from
Make Believe Love
By Jason Warwick

[Friday, June 16th]

By the time Darwin Andrew Goodwin finished the murmuring and halting account of his all-too-brief assignation with Stephanie Rush, the sun had dropped through the horizon, leaving only a slowly fading purple stain on the darkening sky, and in the hollow of the silence after the last word I was left staring at the veil of dust that had collected on my father's dashboard, listening to Goodwin tapping a rhythm on his green workpants with the pen he'd found in the glove compartment. The dust could no longer be seen in the dim light, but earlier, as the story began and the sun flooded through the windshield, it was revealed so clearly that I had slowly drawn my initials in it. To tell the truth, by the time he stopped talking I had actually drifted away, imagining myself spraying the vinyl with vinegar and water and wiping it back to its glorious pebbled cherry finish, so that I entirely missed his final words. I shook my head to rouse myself and he took my gesture as some sort of emphatic response, which started him speaking again.

"That city'll kill her. She's gotta get outa there. But she doesn't see it. She thinks she's safe. She's moved up *there* now, on the side of the San Guanos or Gabriels or whatever you call them. She lives in what they call a 'gated community.' You heard of those?"

I had. It's all part of the American retreat to the medieval, walling themselves up inside tiny city-states with armed guards to keep out the barbarians. To discourage attacks they execute someone every five days. And while they slip into violent paranoia, half of them believing that Elvis is alive and well and running everything from a bunker under the White House—while they slip into collective madness we sit up here just over their northern border, no gates to protect us, hoping they won't notice.

But I'm sounding a little paranoid myself, aren't I? As though we weren't every bit as silly, in our distinctly Canadian ways.

"They think they're safe 'cause they can keep out the niggers and the illegal aliens, but it's not aliens they should be worried about. It's Mother Nature's gonna get 'em. Last year they had to evacuate the entire place when brushfires went through. The chaparral'd got too old. As it ages, it produces this oil, and when it catches on fire it burns like gasoline. Nature's way of cleanin' up after herself. Lightning struck and the mountain went up in smoke. Poof." He stopped tapping the pen on his trousers to make the inferno rise in my mind with a flourish of his hands. "And now there's nothin' holdin' the mountain down, and it's started to rain, and there's gonna be mudslides. And if those don't get them, something else will. Eventually there'll be an earthquake and the whole city'll fall into the ocean."

If they don't run out of water first.

And head north looking for more.

He put the pen back in the glove box and gently snapped the door shut.

There was probably something I should have said, something to placate his terrible fears for the fate of the one he loved, something at once wise and a little bit innocent. Unfortunately, I couldn't think of anything at the time.

"That's all," he broke the silence, reaching for the doorhandle. "I guess you got what you wanted, Joan Swift. Nice that one of us did."

"I won't tell …" I said, and then left it at that, figuring he likely wasn't interested in any more lies.

"I'd better get back to work." He opened the door. "I've wasted the sun."

He got out of the car and slammed the door too hard.

I watched him start his tractor—the engine rattling my windows, the muffler glowing from its spout as if a star were about to rise from the old machine's steel bowels—before I started my car, put it in gear, and drove back over the tracks I'd made as I'd entered the field, over the progression of weedy triangles waiting to be erased by the cultivator's passing. I was thinking about what a feeling that must be, to have squandered the very centre of the solar system and have nothing left but night.

"Hello?"

It was Carol who answered.

"Could I speak to Jason, please."

There was a silence as she considered this request, but at last she called, "Jason, somebody would like to speak to you," in a silly voice that I guess was supposed to be mimicking mine. I heard him ask who it was and her say she had no idea.

"Hello?"

"I've got the tape."

"Pardon?"

"I've got Goodwin's story on tape. He told it to me himself. I didn't have to *use* his mother. Shall I bring it over?"

The line hummed, the faint murmurings of another line interfering with ours: the unrecognizable voices of another conversation going on somewhere else in Broken Head or on the other side of the world. When Jason finally spoke, it was as though he were speaking from that other line, talking from some small town in South Africa or Australia or Malaysia or Japan.

"Yeah, that's fine, I ... uh ... I'll let you know tomorrow."

"No. Let me know now."

He forced out a gargled laugh.

"I don't think that's possible ..."

"It can be erased."

Another silence, the voices on the other line buzzing eloquently, like mosquitoes in a church basement on a Wednesday evening in spring.

"Sure ... well ... uh ... perhaps," Jason stammered. "But I only have a few minutes."

"You've wasted the sun."

He pondered this statement.

"Okay. In a half an hour, then? I'll see you *there*."

And he hung up.

He seemed a wee bit upset when I opened my door.

"What the fuck is wrong with you?"

"Oh, nothing a bullet wouldn't fix. And what, may I ask, is wrong with you?"

Pursing his lips in a way that suggested he was about to spit an answer, he pushed by me and slammed the door to make sure anybody who happened to cruise by would not catch sight of him. My little house was immaculate: magazines displayed tastefully on the coffee table, CDs in their racks, underwear hidden away in its proper drawer, everything neat and tidy, nothing revealed except what I wanted revealed. Jason plopped down on the couch without taking off his jacket.

"I told you never to call my home. You have no right …"

"No," I interrupted him. "Apparently, I don't. But I do have a tape."

I cradled the tiny cassette in the palm of my hand. When he reached for it, I closed my fist. He sighed.

"I'm getting tired of this."

"Are you? Me too. I feel like I could sleep forever." I sat down next to him on the couch, curled up in the corner like I used to do when I was watching cartoons. "You know what I was thinking? I was thinking that when that man gave me these words on this tape, he entrusted me with his story. Trust. You know what that word means?" He didn't answer. "What have you ever given me?"

He sat there grinding his teeth.

"Are you gonna give me the tape or not?"

"I don't know." I scratched my head for an answer. "What are you gonna give me?"

He shrugged graciously.

"You can have every dollar the movie honchos offer. I don't give a rat's ass about the money. All I want is the rights to the tape, so that I can use it for my book."

That fleck of black in his iris.

"No."

He sighed.

"What exactly do you want?"

Thus opening a can of worms I was more than willing to serve up for him.

"Oh, I don't know. Happiness, I guess. Or maybe just some sort of relief from unrelenting pain. Thinking of her sleeping with you every night. Thinking of her fucking you. Do you know what that's like? I'm in constant utter ugly horrible crippling pain. Maybe it would be nice just to be numb. Like you. How do you manage that? What are you taking?"

He sat back into my orange floral bed.

"I'm tired. I'm so tired."

I set the cassette on the coffee table, picked up the remote, and flicked on the television.

"You're losing it, Joan."

"Am I?"

"There's not really anything on that tape, is there?"

"Pardon?"

"Well, let's listen to it then, and see if it's any better than the last one."

Talk show, sitcom, news, evening soap opera: I surfed the channels, catching the drift of each embarrassment, then moving on to the next.

"How did you manage to get this tape?"

"I asked him. He told me."

He slapped his cheeks and held his head so it wouldn't fall off.

"Why didn't I think of that?"

I paused at "The Simpsons," but I'd already seen that one twice.

"Listen, I don't have much time," he said, leaning forward. I snatched up the cassette. He glared, then snorted dismissively.

"Forget it."

Rising to his feet, he began talking down at me, still curled there on the corner of my couch, my bed, a piece of white plastic clutched in one hand, the remote in the other.

"You know what I think? I think there's nothing on that tape. This is just a silly ploy to get me here and watch me twist in the breeze. And I'm tired. I'm just so tired of it all."

I pointed the remote at him and pressed the button. The television blinked off. I suppose the beam must have bounced off his body and done its only job. You couldn't see it bounce. Maybe it's not even a beam. Maybe it's a sound, pitched so high that only the television can hear. To someone dropped from an earlier time it would have seemed magic. Our lives are so filled with magic. Useless magic. Jason was still standing there.

I pulled myself up before him, standing on my tiptoes so that I could look him straight in the eye.

"Is that so?"

I waited for him to say more, but he pressed his lips together and outwaited me.

"There's nothing on it? Well, if that's the case, do you want to watch me smash it?"

He stood there with an expression on his face that could only be interpreted as a challenge.

Dad had given me a red metal tool kit with some basic accessories for Christmas. Older technologies. There was a hammer with a red fibreglass handle. So far I hadn't used it much. I fetched it from the closet, set the cassette on the floor before me and crouched over it with the hammer ready. Jason stood at the door, unable to wipe that look off his face.

"Shall I?"

Slowly, wearily, he shrugged.

"Whatever."

I hammered away until the last substantial fragment of plastic casing spun across the floor and there was nothing but a few shards and a tangled mess of metallic tape. I picked up the tape and started pulling it, stretching it, tearing it, winding it around me in slow whirls as though this were some sort of ritual for a new religion, and I, its vestal virgin, had gods speaking through me. Jason stood grimly watching the entire performance and when I looked up to see if he was satisfied he said, "I knew there was nothing on it."

And he walked out, leaving the door open behind him.

I took a bath—something I do when I've reached my limit. Lolling in the water seems to help me fight off the most oppressive depression. That's what I felt: not anger, but depression. I was drowning in the sudden all-consuming knowledge that I was unloved and unlovable; that no one had ever cared about me or ever would; that no one even knew who I was. Including me. But gradually, as I lay there watching the tap's slow steady drip land on my big toe, I began to feel the truth descending. Jason wasn't going to act unless he was forced. He was too much of a coward.

Yes, that was it! We were living these huge lies—not just Jason and me, but Carol too, and if I were to accomplish one thing in my life it might be to shed a little light on a dark ugly world so that its inhabitants might look around and see the beauty before it swallowed them.

If I had to hurt this much, then Jason should be hurting too.

I stepped from the tub with all the bravado and determination of a warrior Venus emerging from the briny deep. For armour, I donned my yellow dress. It looked good on me. I left the wig hanging on a door handle.

I walked the walk I'd walked a thousand times before, but this time I was actually going there, not just slinking past and glancing over my shoulder to see if anyone had noticed. It wasn't far—only a dozen blocks. Nothing is far in Broken Head.

At moments of truth the world takes on hard edges. Every swirl in the sidewalk is the signature of the man who trowelled it there, every flowerbed is a tangible expression of the woman who plants and tends it, every bird has a heart that beats about a thousand times per minute, and the sun is a round star 93 million miles away. From my tiny perspective the moon had just appeared from behind a house that was built the year I was born—built and occupied by a developer whose daughter was a few years ahead of me in school. Carol, her name was. She was the envy of every other girl when she began to bud breasts in grade six. Her dad was rich, too. He bought her a car for her sixteenth birthday. Wouldn't it be great to have such a wonderful life? In grade twelve she'd had the lead role in the high-school musical. One long fairy tale. And maybe everything would have continued on that magical musical course if her brother hadn't taken that short flight through his windshield. Did one terrible loss set her on the road to tragedy? Could that have been enough to turn her life into one great facade hiding her horrible secret? Jason's wife. She was nobody's wife. It had to be painful, living one long uninterrupted lie. But that was all about to end.

When I got to the Warwick home I stood outside for a few moments, admiring that stuccoed monument to connubial bliss, checking out what I could see of her flowerbeds by the streetlights—the silky petals curled tightly, asleep—trying to summon all of my courage. I could see her through the large picture window, sitting in her living room, reading a book. She might have been you, reader, sitting where you sit right now, looking inside me, except her eyes were so doll-like I'm surprised she could see to the other side of the room. And it wasn't just her eyes, it was everything, right from the watch on her wrist with the white plastic band, to the perfect circles of blush on her pale cheeks. Only her nose was a little large, like the hockey players who've been taken into the boards once too often.

A blue light flickered in the basement window. He'd be watching the news—Peter Mansbridge chanting him off to bed with lullabies of a decaying world. Little did he suspect that the news had escaped his television and was climbing his front steps.

I rang the bell and a moment later Carol answered the door.

"Oh?"

I tried to make sense of the question.

She was still carrying the book.

"What are you reading?" I asked.

"Pardon?"

No, that wouldn't do. I'd have to be more direct.

"My name is Joan Swift. May I come in?"

The way she was looking at me. Something was not right. It wasn't that she was expecting me, but almost.

"There's something I need to talk to you about."

"I … don't think so."

She started to close the door, but I put my foot in the way. She took a step back.

"What do you think you're doing? Do you want me to call the police?"

"I'm sorry, but I really need to talk to you."

A little girl stared over her shoulder from a photograph on the wall behind her. The little girl wore a lacy white dress and carried a bouquet of red flowers.

"Jason's told me all about you," she said.

Her eyes were a terrible blue. The little girl's were brown.

"He has?"

"Yes." She nodded, then added, "Leave us alone."

A disturbingly light blue, like those veins on the insides of Jason's wrist.

"Is that really what *he* wants? Have you asked him that?"

Her nod was severe, her mouth cut by a razor blade, her lips a thin red line matching the girl's terrible flowers.

"I don't believe it. I want to hear it from him. I want us all to talk about it together."

The little girl smiled so sweetly she could not have been real. She must have been some sort of computer-generated image that was downloaded off the Internet and sold framed in card shops. Carol shook her head to show her exasperation.

"Why Jason?"

She'd stolen the photo from one of her show homes.

"I don't know. There must be something about him. Those blue veins. That fleck of black. Why are you with him?"

Her pouty lips curled into a confused and condescending grin.

"He doesn't even know Goodwin, you know? Goodwin won't even talk to him."

She was speaking to a child, the little girl in the photo who, despite the brown eyes, turned out to be me, a decoration for her wall. Or perhaps I was the textured wallpaper.

"It's got nothing to do with Goodwin. Your husband and I have been having an affair for over a year now."

Her smile began slowly to fade as though she were recalling something she'd been trying to forget for more years than she cared to remember.

"Is that so?" She looked me over again, hoping to spy the truth bulging somewhere on my person. "He says you came to him with some plan to get Goodwin's story. He says you're crazy."

"I'm not crazy. I'm telling the truth."

"Really?"

Taunting. Actually daring me to cross her threshold. I put one toe over, testing the nap of her white carpet.

"I want to talk to Jason."

"That's quite a dress. I saw it on the news last night. But you forgot your wig. Do you really believe you're her?"

I drew my foot back.

"I just dress this way for Jason. He likes to pretend I'm her when we make love."

Blue eyes roughly the colour of the sky just over the horizon, and terrible flower-red lips.

"Get out of my house."

I took a step toward her, slowly, as though she were planning to jump from a ledge and I was intent on stopping her.

"I'll call the police," she said.

I took another step forward.

She'd have cut me into tiny fragments if she could, sliced me up so that there was nothing left of me except the odd molecule you might pick up as static on your television if you liked to watch the channels with nothing on. As it was, all she managed was to get a bit of my flesh under her nails. That made me feel better. I touched the marks on my cheek and checked my hand to see that there was blood.

"Get out!" she said.

I realized that Jason must have heard by now, but hadn't bothered or dared to make an appearance. He was hiding somewhere in the bowels of their dream home, waiting for his wife to chase me away. I looked into her eyes one last time, trying to calculate exactly how much she hated me.

"Please, just go away," she said.

And I obeyed.

It occurred to me later that I should have stayed and been arrested. She didn't want the truth to come out, but I had nothing else to offer. The reason I ran was a sudden fear that if I stayed and the police showed up and did their investigation they'd only discover it was Jason who was telling the truth—that he'd never kissed me, that he'd never touched me, that we'd never made love, that my entire miserable life was one long bad dream from which I could never be roused.

When I got home I paced the house in a frenzy of manic energy, talking to myself about what an idiot I was, screaming at my image in the mirror, weeping like a scolded and humiliated child, running my fingers through my hair in a futile attempt to massage my pounding brain through my skull, until—it must have been hours later—I finally managed to cry myself into a great dark tunnel of sleep.

A knock woke me.

I thought at first it was morning, but when I stumbled into the kitchen to splash water on my face and peer out the window I saw by the clock on the stove that it was already past one in the afternoon. Susie was standing on my doorstep with the same two solemn male cousins who had helped move us in. Their grain truck was parked at the curb. Immediately, I opened the door to her even though I was still wearing my yellow dress, and even though it was rumpled and wrinkled in exactly the way it would have been if I'd slept in it.

"Hello," I said.

There was a long silence as she and the cousins studied the evidence of my dress and the scratches on my cheek.

"We're here for my things," Susie finally said.

"You don't have to move out, Susie."

The cousins turned and pretended to appraise their truck, glancing back at my dress every so often, hovering impatiently.

"I'm here for my things. I don't wish to discuss it, thank you very much."

She had on her library clerk demeanour, giving final notice to a patron with a long list of overdues.

"He said he's leaving Carol. He asked me to move to Toronto."

Susie sighed and shook her head.

"Have a nice time. Can I please come in and get my things?"

"He wanted me to make a tape of Goodwin's mother, but I wouldn't do it. I got a tape of Goodwin but I wouldn't even give it to him. I smashed it. I couldn't give it to him."

Susie's only response was to look at her feet. The cousins shifted their eyes back and forth between me and their truck. They looked a little bored, as though they'd heard it all a million times before and were waiting for the good part, when I took off the dress.

I drew in a deep breath and stepped out of their way.

In a very few minutes they had carted out her bed and her dresser and her bookshelf and her desk and the kitchen table. We'd bought the table together, but Susie obviously didn't remember it that way, and I didn't object. She, meanwhile, boxed up her books, picked through the CDs, rifled the kitchen cupboards for her share of the Melmac and stainless steel cutlery, packed up her penguins.

"Could you strip the sheets so they can take the couch," she said, motioning to my orange floral bed.

"Oh," I said. "But aren't the sheets your mother's? Or do you want me to wash them and bring them to you?"

"No, that's fine," she said, pushing the bed back into its hiding place with the sheets still on it, and directing her cousins to haul it away.

"You can have the coffee table," she said. "Will you take a hundred dollars for the television and VCR?"

We'd paid two hundred, splitting the cost.

"No. That's all right. You can have them. You can have the coffee table, too."

She left the hundred dollars on the coffee table in the middle of the empty room.

"See you at work," I called after her as she left. Without so much as a glance back, she closed the door.

An hour later I wandered back into the living room to look at my coffee table and noticed some activity going on in the front yard. A woman with bleached hair was standing on my front lawn talking into a microphone while a small camera crew looked on, digitalizing her for the world with my house as her background. I grabbed some clothes, ran into the bathroom and changed, stuffing the yellow dress into the garbage pail. They were already knocking on the door by the time I'd emerged.

I opened the door a crack.

"Hello?"

"Could I speak to Joan Swift?"

"What do you want?"

The camera was parked at the bottom of my steps, the lens peering up past the woman.

"I was just wondering if you were the woman who came to the courthouse two days ago for the Goodwin trial?"

"No."

"Are you Joan Swift?"

"No."

"You look like her."

I had opened the door two inches too far. She showed me the picture from my grade twelve yearbook.

"What do you want?"

"What sort of relationship do you and Mr. Goodwin have?"

"None. We're just friends."

I opened the door a little farther to emphasize this point.

"Is it true that you and Mr. Goodwin are lovers?"

I sneered for the camera.

"There's never enough love to go around."

I slammed the door closed. They knocked again, and I sat down there with my back against the solid core.

He'd done it. Jason had talked to his friends and made me a star. Something else had happened in Broken Head, that place in Saskatchewan. Joan Swift had happened. I was to be the next Goodwin, or at least an interesting twist in his story. And the story had everything: love, sex, betrayal, penguins. No, the penguins were all gone.

Still, the advertisers would love me.

I decided to kill myself.

I would not leave a note.

At first, I'd considered writing a long epistle laying the blame squarely on Jason's sloped shoulders, but in the end I opted for something more subtle. I knew the lack of documentation to mark the occasion would annoy Susie. She'd always been a model of manners when she left a conversation or the table.

Deciding how to go about it was more difficult. Initially, I thought pills. Wouldn't you? I imagined myself drifting away, sleeping beauty, waiting until the end of time for the kiss that would awaken me. But on second thought that all seemed to be a little too pretty. If I tied a belt to the hook Susie had attached to a beam in her bedroom ceiling—

attached to hang a potted fern—I could kick away the only remaining chair and die that way. You know how it's done. You've probably seen it on television. I even looped the belt up there and tested it to see that it would carry my weight.

But I couldn't do it. I stood there on the chair, staring into the corner above where Susie's bed had been, watching a spider work on a web. The belt was looped through the buckle, and all I had to do was slip it over my head, but it was such a violent thing to act out on the person who I knew would walk through the door: my father. I considered phoning Jason and somehow convincing him to come and find me. I wanted that image of me hanging there burned into his mind, haunting him in the wee small hours of every dark night, no matter whose body he tried to hide in. *Watch this. Live with this for the rest of your life.* It would be his punishment for not returning my love. Even if he couldn't. *Couldn't.* What kind of excuse is that?

But I doubted I could get him come to me again, even one more time. And I finally convinced myself that if I was going to do it it should be in the most dramatic way possible. If this was all that was to become of me, if this was all I was made for, then I'd better make the most of it, and if there was no way of avoiding that image in my parents' minds, I'd burn it into everyone else's, so that the world might remember me for something at least.

I'd have to make it a truly grand statement.

I took the butcher knife out of the kitchen cupboard, put on my wig, got into my father's car, which I was already supposed to have returned, and headed out to Goodwin's farm, where I parked on an approach across the grid and snuck in through the Stephanie Rush Memorial Forest.

The tallest of those pines is still only twenty feet high, though he planted them twenty years ago.

The prefab looked prim and tended, as befitted the house of a couple of newlyweds. I saw no point in subtlety: I kicked the locked door until the frame split.

It was a shrine. Posters of Stephanie Rush covered every wall: there she was in the arms of Burt Reynolds under a gibbous moon, and there she was gazing over the camera as though she'd just caught sight of God Himself moving across the sky, and there she was lying back in the bow of a gondola while a handsome gondolier poled her down a canal burnished in sienna light. A complete library of her films was filed in the slots of the stand under a large-screen television set. A life-sized mannequin of her balanced in a corner of the living room, a bit off kilter, as though she'd had one too many cocktails at the Crocodile Club. The bedroom was an exact replica of the penthouse bedroom in *Blow Me Away*, complete with the round white waterbed, the white shag carpet, and the pink Tiffany lamps. I examined the Stephanie Rush doll sitting on the dresser, thinking that the bed would be the spot to do it, the place to die. I was testing the knife on the blow-up doll's wrists, watching her deflate, when Darwin Andrew Goodwin walked through the doorway.

We stared at one another for about the time it takes to change your mind about something important enough to change the world. I was trying to understand what I saw in his eyes, to resolve it with my expectations, which were, I suppose, violent. Someone had struck me once already only the night before and it made sense that I was about to be hit again. I raised the knife to where he couldn't help noticing it.

"Sorry," I said.

"She's gone," he said.

I looked at the doll, her features deformed by the loss of air.

"Oh," I said.

"The mudslides got the house. Didn't I tell ya? As far as they know she was there. She's missing."

"They'll find her."

"I'm gonna go look."

I dropped the knife.

"What. You're going to California?"

"Yeah. To look for her."

"I wouldn't do that."

"I'm gonna."

"They'll arrest you at the border."

"There's lots of spots to cross. There's lots of places where the border's just a field."

"I wouldn't. What good will it do? How will you find her?"

"I'll find her."

His tone was one of absolute certainty. I sat down on the bed and took off my shoes.

"What do you want me to do?"

It was as though I'd been summoned. He came to the bed and sat down beside me.

"You can stay here. You can look after my mother."

And he dissolved into tears. I took him in my arms and he buried his face in my neck, blubbering while I tried to soothe him, patting his back as if to coax up a stubborn burp, telling him that everything would be okay.

We watched it on CNN an hour later.

When it rained, the slides started, great heaving rivers of mud flowing down toward the filthy city, carrying boulders the size of one of Jupiter's moons in their kinetic charge. As these rivers swept through the shiny new neighbourhoods they picked up debris along the way: trees and trucks and townhouses. It was late morning. Her husband had left her to sleep. The river of mud carried a Rolls-Royce through their bedroom wall. So far, they'd found no body.

That night I dreamed I was her, that her bedroom was our barn, that a Rolls-Royce was chasing me, that I dove under, breathing muck into my lungs. I was dead before I managed to wake up.

Goodwin left the next morning. I tried again to talk him out of it, but it was no use. He gave me complete instructions about how to look after things. At the time, I told myself that that's what saved me. Only a few hours before I'd been certain I wanted to be dead, but now I had a mother to look after.

It was all just a rationalization. Really, I didn't have the courage. Or, if you prefer, I wasn't *that* much of a coward.

I knocked on her door and she opened it much the same way as she had a couple of months before.

"What do *you* want?" she asked.

"Darwin asked me to look after you. While he's gone."

"And how long would *that* be?" she asked.

"I'm not sure."

"Probably forever, then, I would expect."

She looked up into the sky, directly over my head, and I wondered if she'd spotted something up there dropping toward me. I glanced skyward, but there was only blue.

"I don't think it'll be that long," I said.

"But you have no answers. Remember?"

"What do you want me to do?"

She sighed and cast her eyes around the yard to take in all of the chores that needed done.

"The seeding. Somebody will have to do the seeding."

And she closed the door in my face.

Mother came for a visit last night, which I suppose is a bit of a breakthrough, though I don't see her being back again very soon. I had told Mrs. Goodwin—her given name is Ethel, but I can't imagine calling her anything but Mrs. Goodwin—that my mother would be here for supper, and she prepared accordingly, though she is still angry with me for locking myself up in my office a whole week and not doing a lick of work. The cultivating is done and the calves are castrated and inoculated and the bulls have been let out to service the cows and Dad is changing the teeth on the new mower he bought at an estate auction for twenty dollars. The new mower was manufactured in 1957.

Dad was out by the shop last night, checking over his purchase, when Mom drove into the yard and stepped out of her Mazda in an orange dress she'd obviously made herself. Some expert had told her that orange was her colour. Her camera was slung around her neck.

"She's here," I warned Mrs. Goodwin.

I was feeling guilty about how artless and awful I was to you in yesterday's entry, a penitent attitude I thought was appropriate to meeting my mother, so I confidently walked out the door in time to see Dad stride up to Mom and she allow him to give her a quick peck on the cheek.

"As lovely as ever," Dad said.

"Thank you," Mother answered, studying his work clothes. "Have I overdressed?"

"Always," Dad said.

"I thought I was told dinner."

"You look great. I just haven't got around to my bath yet."

"You? Bathe?"

By this time I was giving her a hug that felt stiffer and more mechanical than I'd meant it to be.

"Hello, dear."

She looked around her, at the old machinery and the trees, trying her best not to appear too judgemental. "So this is what the two of you are up to."

I pointed to the camera.

"What's that for?"

"I haven't seen you in a while. I thought I might want a few pics."

"Oh," I said. "Shall we go inside?"

"I'll be in in a minute," Dad said.

Mother nodded and, girding herself for the effort, marched along with me to the front door.

"The flowers are lovely. Are you keeping the flowers?"

"No. Mrs. Goodwin likes to do it."

Mrs. Goodwin opened the door.

"Come in, come in," she said insistently, as if we were hours late. "Everything's ready. Just find yourself a place."

"Thank you," Mother said, as she followed her into the dining room, which is separated from the kitchen only by a little half wall that backs the kitchen cupboards. Mrs. Goodwin went straight to the oven and fetched the bird, which she'd already carved. She was back to the table before

Mom and I'd had a chance to sit down.

"Where's Dandy?" Mrs. Goodwin said.

"He'll be right in," I told her.

"Well, he'd better hurry it up or it'll all be cold," she scolded, placing the platter in the centre of the table and heading back for more.

"Dandy?" Mom asked, setting her camera on the table beside her plate.

"I used to cook for twenty men at threshing time, and when the time came to eat they'd be at the table or they'd go hungry," Mrs. Goodwin was still talking as she fetched the fresh green beans and the salad. "Sit down, sit down!" she urged, and Mom did as she was told.

Mrs. Goodwin looked Mother over, forming an opinion of the orange dress that she never shared with us.

"How are things in Venus?" she asked.

"Venus? I'm not from Venus."

"Oh," Mrs. Goodwin said, already marching back to the kitchen. "I thought I read somewhere you were."

You know the rest of Goodwin's story. Dandy's story. I won't go into it, except to say that I want him free, that this obsession that he killed Stephanie Rush when she obviously died in a mudslide is every bit as insane as he and I are supposed to be. No, I don't know how he managed to discover her body when no one else could. Some sort of sixth sense, I guess. Or maybe she called him and told him where she'd leave it. That would be something, wouldn't it, if she'd made an effort to leave her body to him?

The point is that she wasn't murdered, and even if she was murdered, he couldn't have done it because he was here when she disappeared. Isn't that clear enough?

But still he sits there in a maximum-security institu-
tion, every bit as guilty as Charles Manson or Jeffrey
Dahmer in the eyes of a public that suddenly adores
Stephanie Rush again because she had the great career
sense to die.

And in their own twisted way I suppose they adore
Darwin Andrew Goodwin too: a Great Canadian Plains
goat with a gigantic rack of gnarled horns; a sacrifice to the
gods of Hollywood. A team of lawyers spend their lives
working for his release—when you bought this diary you
invested in the Darwin Andrew Goodwin Defence Fund—
but all he'll do for himself is tell them to hurry up and kill
him. He confesses. He killed Stephanie Rush.

Does that mean he's less of a coward than I am?

I don't think so.

His mother doesn't think so, either.

My mother ate little and said less. As Mrs. Goodwin was
carrying her plate away, Mom suddenly turned to me and
forced a huge saccharine smile.

"Did you hear that Susie is getting married?"

I fiddled with my dessert fork, trying to process this news.

"No," Dad piped up. "Who's the lucky guy?"

"Oh, you wouldn't know him. He's new to town. He's a
young minister at the United Church."

"What happened to the lady minister—Reverend …
Porter?"

"Oh, I'm not sure. She left. Apparently the congregation weren't happy with her. Her ideas were a little … too
liberal."

"Uh-huh," Dad said. "Well, that's great to hear about Susie. Isn't it, Joan?"

"Yes. I'm very happy for her."

Mrs. Goodwin was back with the dessert: hot apple pie and a gallon pail of vanilla ice cream.

"How's the crop looking on the MacLeod place, Dandy?" she asked as she began cutting the pie.

"A bit patchy," Dad said. "The weeds got too much of a head start."

"His name is not Dandy," my mother said.

Mrs. Goodwin stopped slicing the pie to stare at Mom.

"He is not your son," my mother said.

Mrs. Goodwin picked up her pie lifter and began serving.

"My son?" she said. "No. My son is locked up. My son is a murderer."

She scooped out some ice cream and set the plate down firmly in front of Mom.

"That's not true," Dad said. "He's just a little ... mixed up."

It wasn't long after Dandy was locked up—almost a year ago now—I was out summerfallowing the MacLeod place, the same field he'd been doing the day I drove out wearing my Stephanie Rush dress, when my dad drove up in his car. I was wearing green workpants and a green shirt and a cap I'd been given by a man from the herbicide company that had manufactured the gas the Nazis had used at Auschwitz. Dandy had sent orders from his cell that I was not to listen to the man, and under no circumstances should I waste his hard-earned cash on chemicals. With no herbicide the wild oats had gotten so far ahead of me that they were clogging up the cultivator shanks, and I had to stop every round to untangle things. There I was, yanking away at those tendrils of wild oats, when Dad's car drove up beside the outfit. He got out and came over and started tearing weeds from the shanks I hadn't got to yet.

"Mess," he said.

When all of the shanks were clear I climbed back on the tractor and he climbed up behind me to ride and inspect my progress.

"Mother's worried about you," he shouted into my ear.

"Is she?" I shouted back.

And he nodded.

"Since when does she tell you what she worries about?" I asked, but he couldn't hear me and didn't answer. He didn't even seem to be trying to listen. He was staring at something on the edge of the field. I looked to see what it was. The day before, as I'd started the field, a camera crew had come and set up and taken footage of me driving by on my tractor. But there was no camera crew today.

Finally he pointed at a blond patch in a bluff of dying mustard, and he leaned close to my ear.

"Coyote," he said.

Immediately after finishing her pie, Mother slung her camera back around her neck and announced that she had to be going.

"All right. Well, no standing on ceremony here. I'm used to people eatin' and runnin'," Mrs. Goodwin said, scooping up the dirty dishes and rushing them off to the sink.

Dad and I walked Mom to the car, filling in her silence with our own awkward comments on how lovely an evening it was. The crickets were already out. At the car, she turned and hugged me and began to weep softly. I held her, and Dad stood there kicking the dirt.

"How can you do this?" she asked us. "Can't you see how … twisted this all is?"

"I don't see anything twisted," I said.

"Well, then what would you call it?"

"I don't know. Home?"

"Don't worry about us," Dad said. "We're doing all right here. The crops look good."

And she wept some more.

When she drove away she hadn't taken a single photograph.

The other night I watched Jason on that new Canadian late night talk show hosted by the cop who became a comedian. Mr. Warwick was promoting his book, talking about Dandy and me.

"I wonder what it is they see in each other?" the former cop asked. "Do you think they have much in common?"

"Yeah, they're both crazy," Jason answered and, on cue, the studio audience laughed.

"But is it *true* love?" the comedy cop asked, and they laughed even louder.

This time when I pressed the button Jason did disappear. Maybe it's not such a useless magic after all.

I read he left Carol. Rumour has it he's sleeping with an aspiring model who's really only another bad example.

Mrs. Goodwin has the bedroom in the basement, the way Dandy'd always intended, except he wouldn't allow her to move in until Stephanie Rush came to stay. Dad's room is the one Dandy'd meant for himself, and mine is the master bedroom, where I'd momentarily planned to die.

Has Dad replaced Dandy? He farms the way Dandy always did, using ancient equipment to keep us out of the pockets of the banks and the machinery companies, and using only manure for fertilizer and no herbicides or pesticides or terminal seeds, to keep us out of the clutches of the chemical pushers. He even changed a broken insulator on the phone line Dandy built between our house and the old place. There's no one in the old house to call—no one except the ghosts—but Dandy built that line as a living monument to prairie history, so Dad keeps it in fine order. Does that mean he's tried to replace Darwin Andrew Goodwin, or does it mean he's tried to reinvent himself by learning from the mistakes he made in his first incarnation as a farmer?

I have certainly not replaced Stephanie Rush, as Jason would have it. Our house is just a house now, not a shrine. I've put all of the relics of Stephanie Rush away, stored them in boxes in the basement in case Dandy comes home one day and wants them. We have a kitchen and living room and bedroom and bathroom with all of the normal things that one finds in kitchens and living rooms and bedrooms and bathrooms everywhere. I have an office and a desk where I'm writing this to you now.

And I'm not lying when I tell you that I've finally found true love here.

No. Not with Goodwin.

With *you*.

This is my pearl. I've worried over it long enough now, for a whole long week, and now it's Friday night and time to rest, and so I offer it to you. Please, keep it safe.

As you read these words they enter your mind in a way that makes us more intimate than physical lovers could ever hope to be. I am inside you, just as you exist inside me. You will never be any closer to anyone than you are to me right now.

But aren't I lonely, you wonder? How can I be happy making love to a page? Haven't I turned away from the world for an imaginary life and set up house inside my head?

No. I have a lover living right here with me. I'm engaged to the world. In the mornings, now that it's summer, I sometimes get up at half past three and drive back to the farm I grew up on and sit there by the barn and watch the sun pull itself over the edge of the valley. And, my God, that sun is round.

That's the best I can do.

Can you, crazy or not—can you do any better?

Oh. And I wanted to tell you, finally, just to make my message very old-fashioned and clear: when it comes to love there are only two answers.

No.

Or *Yes.*

Special thanks to

Janice Dexter, Jack Hodgins, Caroline Heath, Steve Noyes, Terry Jordan, Alison Hahn, Mom and Dad, Heather (for teaching me to read), Raymond, Alison, Norman and all the rest of the extended and extensive Gowan family.

The author also wishes to acknowledge the generous support and encouragement of the Saskatchewan Arts Board, the Canada Council, the Ontario Arts Council, Phyllis Nakonechny, Diane Yee, Sharon Butala, Else Marie de Pauw, Donna Costley, Barb and Neil McCrie, Ted Dyck, Lois Simmie, Chris Fisher, Sharon and Glenda McFarlane, Brenda Niskala, David Carpenter, Bonnie Burnard, Joe Rosenblatt, Alison Skelton, Tim Chizik, Ed Wall, Chris Gudgeon, Ralph Stoerzer, Lou Reed, Cynthia McLaren, Jerry Newman, Robert Harlow, George McWhirter, Paul Wilson, Deanna Greunding, Martha Gould, Di Brandt, Heidi Harms, Rob Forsyth, Dianne Warren, Elizabeth Philips, Mary Howes, Carol Jones,

Tillen Bruce, Judy Nelson, Anne Slade, Doris Bircham, Liz Gordon, David Brownridge, Hugh Henry, David Humphries, all of my co-workers at the Chinook Regional Library, and all of my co-players in the Stationery Ramblers and Frayed Knot.

And thanks for their encouragement and their commentary on the work in progress to Janine Cheeseman, Tricia Fish, Su Rynard, Boris Rodriguez, Chris Grismer, Shaun Cathcart, Claire Ross Dunn, Shelley Eriksen, Tecca Crosby, Paul Fox, Karla Heisterberg, Alayna Munce, Jennifer Kuwaja, Julia Sereny, Elke Town, Sally Catto, Jennifer Barclay, Leslie Grant, Hilary Stanley, Lorne and Sherri Kulak, Sharon Brooks, Hadley Obodiac, and special thanks to Diane Martin and Michael Mouland.

My sincerest apologies to everyone I've neglected to mention.

Lee Gowan grew up on a farm in Swift Current, Saskatchewan. He has published short stories and poetry in numerous periodicals and anthologies, including *Canadian Fiction Magazine, Grain* and *Prairie Fire,* and was twice nominated for The National Magazine Awards. He currently teaches writing at the University of Toronto's School of Architecture. He lives in Toronto with his wife and their young son.